DEAD JEALOUS

A gripping crime thriller full of twists

HELEN H. DURRANT

JOFFE BOOKS

Published 2017 by Joffe Books, London.

www.joffebooks.com

This book is a work of fiction. Names, characters, businesses, organizations, places and events are either the product of the author's imagination or are used fictitiously. Any resemblance to actual persons, living or dead, events or locales is entirely coincidental. The spelling is British English.

ISBN- 978-1-912106-88-2

For my gorgeous grandchildren — Imogen, Jake, Layla, Holly and Evie.

Prologue

She looked him straight in the eyes. "C'mon then, hand it over."

In her high heels, the girl stood slightly taller than him. She had her hands on her skinny hips, daring him to default on their deal. "Ain't got the balls, have yer? Knew it!" She tossed back her long hair. "You're like all the rest, a bloody loser."

She could tell he was afraid. She saw it in his eyes, the way they kept darting back and forth between her and the black shadows cast by the tower blocks.

"Scared someone's watching us?" she taunted. "Afraid someone's waiting out there ready to pounce, are yer?" She moved closer until her face was only centimetres from his. "I ask you to do one simple thing. You're a waste of space, do you know that?" She'd had enough. Turning her back on him, she walked away towards the shadows.

"No!" he shouted after her. "I've got the stuff. I just wanted to be sure."

She stopped and half turned. "Sure of what? That I won't tell anyone?"

"I've not done this before," he said quietly.

She shook her head. "I'm calling time. I was an idiot for asking you in the first place."

"But I need the money!"

"Tough!" She spun round and watched him, a sly smile on her face. She pulled a roll of notes from her jeans pocket, held them aloft and waved them, taunting. "Pity. You could have had a lot of fun with this little lot."

"I'm not lying. I have got the stuff. But not here."

"Follow me." She walked into the shadows, knowing that he would follow. "Some dealer you're going to make."

"Here. This what you want?"

She snatched the packet from him, a big grin on her face. "Good boy! I got it wrong, didn't I? I might even use you again." She stuffed the drugs into the pocket of her leather jacket, leaned forward and kissed his cheek. "Now, do one."

"What about my money?"

"Get lost! Treat this as a lesson in customer satisfaction. If I'm satisfied," she patted her pocket, "I might pay you. But if not . . ." She spun round and walked away.

"You can't do this! I got what you wanted. I took all the risks."

She could hear him trotting up behind her. He was like all the rest, an idiot, easily taken in. She'd never had the slightest intention of parting with hard cash.

"Leave me alone or I'll talk," she threatened. "Want everyone to know what you're really like?"

He stopped in his tracks and shouted after her. "You're a selfish bitch, Flora Appleton. You won't get away with this!"

"I already have," she chuckled. "You're so easy to con. Far too trusting, that's your problem."

He was no better than all the rest. Which was a shame, because Flora quite liked him. If he had shaped up, they could have had fun together. She walked away. There was business to be taken care of. She had money in her pocket and drugs to sell. She heard the footsteps again. He was back. She turned to look, but there was no one.

She shouted at the shadows. "Don't play games with me!" Flora squinted into the darkness. There was a slight movement beside a row of bins several metres away. He was following her. Wants his money, she supposed. She smiled to herself. That wasn't going to happen.

"I know you're there," she called out. "You'll have to try a lot harder if you want spook me."

Flora turned into an alley that ran between two of the tower blocks. It was within sight of the Pheasant pub, which was lit up like a beacon. He wouldn't have the nerve to follow her here. Too scared of being seen. She strolled past the pub, hands in her pockets and began to whistle. Maybe she would finish the night off in the pub.

Suddenly someone grabbed at her arms and pulled her off balance. Flora staggered, and teetered on her high heels. She tried to turn, to shove her assailant away, but a blow to the head put paid to that. She fell to the ground.

Flora Appleton lay face down on the concrete. Greedy hands tore at her jacket, went through the pockets, and found the drugs and the roll of notes.

Flora wriggled a few inches forward, trying to push herself up. He had more balls than she'd given him credit for. Then she cried out. Her assailant yanked her head up by the hair, and slammed her face hard into the concrete. Flora groaned, and spat out a mouthful of blood. As soon as she could, she caught her breath, and screamed for all she was worth.

"No you don't, bitch." The jolt of another blow to the back of her head. But she'd wriggled onto her side and was able to lash out. Her fist made contact with flesh. She was howling and swearing. Then she felt the first sting of the blade.

It slashed across her thigh.

She heard, 'Shut up! Shut up! Shut up!' screamed over and over. The knife struck again. And again, delivering searing pain to different parts of her body. Flora knew the only way she would survive this was by attracting serious attention.

She gave another piercing scream and kicked out frantically. She was running out of time. She tried to turn, push the bastard off, and flipped onto her back. Wild eyes bored into hers, filled with anger and hate. Seconds later the blade entered deep inside her chest. Flora Appleton lay still.

Chapter 1

Nine days later — Monday

It was three in the morning and Detective Tom Calladine was weary. He'd been fast asleep when the call came. The incident was serious, and he had no choice but to attend. The body of a teenage girl had been found stuffed in the boot of a car on the Hobfield.

"You're not going to like it," Natasha Barrington warned. "Stinks to high heaven."

A CSI lifted the boot lid and stood aside. Natasha hadn't been joking. The smell and the sight were dreadful. What was left of the girl was curled up. The horror of it was that her body had been bent and twisted to fit into the small space.

Natasha shook her head. "All that hot weather we've been having has muddied the waters, I'm afraid. Decomposition is well advanced. We'll have to be careful just getting her out of there."

Calladine's imagination ran riot, calling up images of limbs dropping off as they lifted her. He shook himself. It was the double whiskey he'd had before bed, and the tiredness. There was no point in asking if anyone recognised her. As she was now, she was barely recognisable as human.

"Bus pass. No name, I'm afraid — too well worn. But it's one of the sixteen to eighteen ones. So a college student, I'd say." Natasha smiled.

He turned to Roxy Atkins, one of the Duggan's senior forensics people who'd also attended, and mumbled, "Let me have an ID as soon as. Nothing more I can do here."

He felt sick. The smell, the sight . . . he hadn't been prepared. Tiredness notwithstanding, he had the wit to realise that this was a nasty one. Someone had killed that girl, then left her to rot. Whoever had done that needed catching.

"The lads who found her are over there." Natasha pointed to a group of shocked-looking youngsters huddled together by a wall.

"I'll have a quick word." Calladine beckoned to a uniformed officer. "Come with me and take their statements."

* * *

Calladine woke up later that morning feeling as if he'd spent half the night on the Hobfield estate. In actual fact, he'd been there less than an hour. His bones ached and he couldn't stop yawning. Once he had been able to take a broken night's sleep in his stride. That was fast becoming a thing of the past.

He cleaned the incident board and made a neat list of the meagre details they had. Soon the photos would be on the police computer system. They'd be printed out and pinned up here too. That should focus the minds of his colleagues when they got to the office.

Natasha Barrington from the Duggan Centre (where all the forensics and pathology were now outsourced to) had already phoned. She'd been at it since the early hours. With careful cleaning, the student bus pass had revealed the victim's surname. That and the fact that the victim was a student had helped with tracing dental records. Fortunately the local dentist was able to find a match quickly. Dental records confirmed that the body was that of sixteen-year-old Flora Appleton. Now they knew for sure, Calladine had the unenviable task of telling Flora's mother. He'd take Ruth with him. She was better at the morbid stuff than him. She always knew the right thing to say. Then he remembered — it was Ruth's morning off.

"There's a woman downstairs asking to see you, guv."

Calladine looked up from his desk and gave DC Nigel Hallam a quizzical look. The young detective was first to arrive and smartly dressed, as always. He had that eager, 'keen to do well' expression on his face. It was starting to grate. "Do we know what she wants?"

"No, but she asked specifically for you. Said it was important, she'd talk to no one else, and she'd wait."

Calladine was trying to sort out the witness statements gathered last night regarding the Flora Appleton case. The kids who'd found her in the boot of that car had been traumatised and he wasn't surprised that their statements made little sense. But they all agreed that Flora hadn't been seen around for a little over a week. After collecting their statements, Calladine had left it to the CSIs and the team from the Duggan to remove the body. He was relieved not to have to witness that little operation.

Given how and where the girl had been found, the death was obviously suspicious. They'd know more once the post-mortem had been carried out and the CSIs had done their work. For a start, it would be helpful if they knew exactly where the girl had been killed. Flora had been missing for a full week, but her mother had not reported it. Calladine was having difficulty with this anomaly.

"Did she say if it had anything to do with Flora Appleton?" The young DC shook his head. "Okay, I'll pop down and have a word."

The main office was unusually empty. His sergeant, Ruth Bayliss, had the morning off. DC Simon Rockliffe — Rocco to his mates — was on an IT course in some far-flung corner of Wales. Calladine took the stairs, thinking about his depleted team. Rocco had been 'Rocco' for so long now they were in danger of forgetting his real name! DC Nigel Hallam was new. He'd been a uniformed PC, recently promoted to detective constable and assigned to Calladine's team. Calladine hadn't got the measure of him yet. Nigel had the makings of a good detective, but there was something about him that neither Calladine nor the rest of the team had taken to. The lad had a steep hill to climb. It was hard to have to fill the void left by the death of Imogen Goode. Perhaps that was it.

The team were all painfully aware that Nigel wouldn't be with them at all if Imogen hadn't been killed. Calladine still got upset when he thought of the pretty DC. It had happened three months ago, but it was still very raw, particularly with Ruth. She'd not been herself since.

The woman who'd asked to see him was pacing the floor in the small room next to the reception area. Calladine didn't recognise her. He put her at roughly forty. She was small with short spiky hair, and dressed in jeans and a baggy sweater. She was holding something wrapped in a small blanket.

He greeted her with a smile. "Can I help?"

"Jill Hodge." She smiled back. "I came to give you this. I think it might be important." She handed him the item she'd been carrying. "I've moved into a house on Beardsell Terrace, number two. I'm about to have a wood burner installed, and I found this bricked up behind the old fireplace."

Wrapped in a child's pink blanket was a small pottery urn, a ginger jar perhaps. It was about twelve inches high and glazed a rich, deep red.

He looked at it, puzzled. "Is it valuable?"

"Possibly," she replied. "But it's what's inside that bothered me."

Calladine lifted the lid and peered inside. "It looks like ash."

"Exactly what I thought." She gave a shudder. "At first I thought the thing must be an urn, and that I'd stumbled upon some poor soul's remains. But now I'm not so sure. I still think they are someone's ashes, but the blanket is a child's." She paused, and drew her lips into a thin line. "This was lying on top, just under the lid." She handed him a second object. "I wrapped it in the tissue paper to keep it safe. I thought it best when I saw what it was." She took a deep breath. "I know the story. I've been away for a while, but I used to live around here."

The wrapping was protecting a child's hairslide. Calladine blinked in disbelief. It was a simple rectangle of pink plastic with a large gold butterfly at one end. Across the length of the topside was printed the name 'Jessica.' Calladine's stomach did a somersault. For a second, he thought he was dreaming. How many times had he looked at an image of this item? For weeks, the hairslide and its owner had stared back at him from the front pages of both the local and national press.

"It's hers, isn't it? And those," Jill Hodge nodded at the ashes, "that's what's left of little Jessica Wilkins."

The colour drained from Calladine's face. She might be right. And if she was . . . ? This would be huge. The press would be all over it — again. Not to mention what it would do to Jessica's mother. But more important to Calladine was the question of what they had missed during the original investigation. If this was indeed Jessica, it meant she'd been kept and killed somewhere local.

He looked at Jill Hodge as if through a fog. "We can't be sure. There will have to be tests."

"How long is it since the child disappeared, about fifteen years?" she asked.

Calladine was feeling queasy. "Seventeen years, five months and a couple of weeks." He saw the quizzical look she gave him. "I still have a copy of the file in my desk drawer." He was slightly embarrassed at this admission. It made it appear that he'd been counting off the days. "I read through the case notes regularly," he added.

"You were part of the investigation team at the time. I remembered your name from the papers. Are you alright? You've gone awfully pale."

Was it any wonder? It was one of the worst cases he'd ever worked on. A missing child, no leads, not even rumours. But worst of all was the fact that the body had never been found. Calladine hated failure, particularly when it involved children. Not finding Jessica, or what had happened to her, hadn't been easy to live with. For weeks he had woken in the dead of night, thinking about the numerous things that could have befallen Jessica. He'd theorised, gone over the events in his head, and retraced the girl's steps until he was worn out. Everything, including all the emotion surrounding that case, was seared onto his brain.

Jessica Wilkins had been nearly two years old. Her mother, Josie, had taken her to Leesdon Park to play. It had been a hot afternoon. She'd left the child sleeping in a pushchair under a tree while she went for an ice cream from the van parked up near the swings. Josie reckoned she'd been away five minutes tops. When she got back, Jessica was gone. Someone had taken her, along with the small pink blanket from her pushchair. The child was never seen again. This was every parent's nightmare, and her mother was beyond frantic. No one had seen anything, there'd been no CCTV. There was absolutely nothing to work with. The investigation lasted months. But inevitably the case was wound down. It remained unsolved.

"We turned this town inside out." Calladine was staring out of the window at the High Street. It was as if time had slipped backwards. He could recall every detail.

"There was no time off for weeks. We searched everywhere. We sent divers into the canal, the river and the reservoir up in the hills. We went house to house, more than once. We went into every cellar in this town. But we got no leads. No one knew anything. All the work we put in was for nothing. It was if the little lass had simply evaporated into thin air."

"You'll want to come to the house?" She touched his arm.

Calladine turned to her and nodded. "There'll have to be a search. Forensics will be heavily involved. I'm afraid they'll more than likely make a mess."

"No worries. I'm up to my eyes in plaster and rubble anyway."

"I'll get it organised. Thank you for bringing these to us. For not simply thinking they were junk and slinging them in the bin."

"I was curious. I thought it was ashes when I saw the container, so no way could I do that. The jar is old, you know, Royal Doulton Flambé Ware. Quite collectable."

* * *

Calladine went straight to acting DCI Brad Long's office. He was sitting at Rhona Birch's desk, shuffling papers and stuffing toast into his mouth. "Hate this bloody job," he spluttered at Calladine. "Birch should get a medal for sorting all this crap every week."

"Do you recall the Jessica Wilkins case?"

Long stopped shuffling. "Course I do. I'm not a completely heartless bastard, you know." He looked up. "Years ago. Kid went AWOL from Leesdon Park and was never seen again."

Calladine sighed. To the point, he supposed, if a little reductive. Long hadn't worked the case, so was not privy to the heartache the others had suffered. "I think her ashes have turned up." Calladine put the ginger jar on the desk.

"Watch it! That's my breakfast," Long blustered, and moved the plate of toast and mug of tea to one side.

"A woman brought it in. She found it wrapped in this blanket here. It was bricked up behind the fireplace of a house she's renovating."

Long peered into the jar. "Then again, this stuff could be anything. Chunky, aren't they?" He gave the jar a little shake. "When my granny was cremated we scattered her up by the res on the Huddersfield Road. Her ashes were pale grey and very fine."

"Careful or they'll be that many different sets of prints on the thing, it'll take forensics an age to sort." Calladine moved the jar out of Long's reach. "If this is Jessica, then whoever burned her would not have had quite the same facilities as the crematorium, would they, Brad? In any case, that will help. Forensics will need any pieces of bone or teeth they can find, in order to prove identity conclusively."

Long shuddered. "Come on then, what makes you think it's her?"

"This." Calladine showed him the hairslide. "This and Jessica's clothing were well documented at the time. Plus the blanket. Apparently the child couldn't sleep without it." He picked it up. The colour had faded over time but it still had the appliqued gold teddy on one corner. "This is exactly as Josie Wilkins described."

"In that case, better get it to the Duggan pronto. Are you going to tell the parents?"

Calladine hadn't thought that far ahead. Jessica had lived with her mother, Josie. Her father, whoever he was, hadn't been around since Josie told him she was pregnant. He knew Josie Wilkins still harboured hopes of her little girl turning up alive. This would take her right back to that dreadful time. Rake it all up again.

Long nodded slowly. "You'll have to tell her. The Duggan will need a DNA sample."

"There will be samples from the original investigation."

Long indicated the slide and blanket. "Even so, DNA from that lot in there will take a while," he nodded at the ash. "She'll have to identify the items before we even begin."

"What if this is some elaborate hoax? Someone playing with Josie's emotions? The woman is delicate, she has been since it happened."

"Tell the woman, Tom," insisted Long. "You can't protect her. One loose word and the press will be all over this like a plague of locusts. We definitely don't want her finding out that way."

Long was right. Calladine would go to the Duggan, drop off the objects, and then go round to the Wilkins home on the Hobfield.

"How are you doing with the Flora Appleton case? Shouldn't you be out on the Hobfield, wringing answers out of the lot of them?"

"We've made a start, Brad. Uniform are going door to door, asking where Flora was seen last. I'll be back there myself later."

"Want Thorpe to lend a hand?"

No, he didn't! They might be short-handed with Rocco missing, but Thorpe would be more of a hindrance than a help. Apart from which, Ruth couldn't stand the bloke. "We'll be fine, thanks. Ruth is back this afternoon. By then we'll know what we're looking at."

"One thing's for certain, the kid didn't climb into that boot and die all by herself," Long said with a sigh. Calladine got up to go. "Birch will be back any day," added Long. "Getting a flight later this week."

"She found her son, then?"

Rhona Birch had taken compassionate leave to chase after her son, who'd gone missing in Australia.

"Took a while. Apparently he'd taken off with some girl he'd met. She found him in Queensland, in some resort, soaking up the sun."

Calladine smiled. "She'll have loved that."

Chapter 2

Ruth Bayliss was in a café on the High Street, drinking coffee with Dr Sebastian Hoyle. He'd rung and asked to meet up. He'd done so a number of times since Imogen's death. He was still concerned about the team, and wanted to hear how everyone was doing after that dreadful event.

Imogen Goode had been killed a few months ago, while working on a case She'd taken off on her own after receiving information she considered important. Unfortunately it proved to be her undoing. She was attacked and killed. The team was left devastated by her loss.

Ruth understood Doc Hoyle's concern. He knew them all well, particularly her and Tom. Before the days of the Duggan Centre and the outsourcing of pathology and forensics, it had been Doc Hoyle and Julian Batho who'd always looked after the team's needs. When Leesdon police began to use the Duggan, Doc Hoyle retired. Some retirement! He was now working flat out as a locum at the health centre.

Ruth liked talking to the doc. It helped her to get stuff off her chest. It was a bit like counselling, but with a friend. After what had happened to Imogen, Ruth felt she needed a bit of therapy. Imogen's death was still a definite no-go topic in the incident room.

"How's Tom doing?" Hoyle asked.

Ruth smiled. "You know what he's like. He pretends that we're all carrying on as normal, but it's tearing him up inside. I've known him a long time, and we've been through a lot together. He keeps all the emotional stuff well hidden. He's doing the *brave face* thing for our benefit. But in many ways it might be better to have a talk, a bloody good weep, and get it all out."

"You're a good team, Ruth. It'll come right. The way you're feeling, the way Tom is, it's a natural reaction. What happened to Imogen was dreadful. Her death has hit the team hard. It is going to take a while."

He was right. The last three months had been difficult. "Stupid, I know, but I still expect to see her sitting there at her computer like she always was. I've had to bite my tongue several times. I've found myself wanting to ask where she's got to. Rocco is just about holding it together. He's not his usual happy self, nowhere near. He's gone off to Wales on an IT course. Not that he needs the training. He was just glad to get away, if only for the change of scenery."

Doc Hoyle nodded. "What about Tom and you?"

"There is no Tom and me. We work together. He's a mate and we're close. Nothing else."

"He kissed you. You don't talk about it anymore, but you did tell me at the time. It rattled you."

"History, Doc. Now let it drop. He's far too old for me, for a start."

Ruth didn't want all that raked up. It was embarrassing. The doc was making a mountain out of a simple gesture. She and Tom had been utterly shocked at finding Imogen like that. It was the particular situation, and way off the scale of what was normal behaviour for both of them.

The doc smiled. "He goes out with women your age all the time. He's not bad looking either. Perhaps that kiss jolted something."

"You think I secretly want an affair with Tom Calladine? That I'm even refusing to admit it to myself?" Her eyes widened. "That's utter rubbish. Where would it leave me and Jake, for a start?"

"How *are* you and Jake?"

She turned slightly, avoiding his gaze. "At each other's throats mostly," she confessed with a sigh. "It's become obvious to me that Jake considers his career far more important than mine. He does less and less around the house or with Harry. These days the little lad could be forgiven for wondering who Jake is!"

"The blip in your relationship will have a lot to do with the strain you've been under of late."

She frowned. "If ever you decide to give up general practice, there's a career waiting for as a psychologist. I'm not daft, I've considered that, but there's more to it."

He took hold of her hands. "I'm your friend, Ruth, and I'm very fond of both of you. Cut Jake some slack. Talk to him."

"I would do that happily if he'd talk back."

"I'm sure he loves you, Ruth. Try a little harder."

At that moment, Ruth's mobile rang. It was Calladine. She cursed under her breath. "I'm supposed to be off this morning."

"A body has been found on the Hobfield. A teenage girl. She was left in the boot of a car to rot. But apart from that, I've got a tricky one and could do with some help."

Ruth rolled her eyes at the doc. "Tricky in what way, Tom?"

"You won't remember. It was before your time. But seventeen years ago a little girl went missing from Leesdon Park. The child was never found. Someone's brought in a pot of ashes and objects which I recognise as belonging to her. They need dropping off at the Duggan, and then I've got to go and tell her mother."

"And you want me to come along and hold the hankie?"

"Josie Wilkins and the teenage girl's mother both live in Heron House. I thought we could speak to both of them. It might have happened years ago, but giving Josie Wilkins the news will be every bit as difficult as telling Dolly Appleton that we've found her daughter's body. Josie is going to take it hard. She's been living in hope all this time. Like any mother, she will never have given up hope. But this is going to make it all fresh again. Fresh and final."

"All this time, and she thought the child was still alive?"

"Yes, I think she did."

"Okay, pick me up on the High Street. I'll wait in the library car park."

* * *

Ruth got into the car beside Calladine. She wasn't smiling.

Calladine looked at her. "I wouldn't have rung but I need you with me on this. The Flora Appleton case has priority, but the Jessica thing needs sorting too. The investigation into the child's disappearance will be reopened, so you need to be up to speed. Plus, Josie Wilkins will be shocked that proof of Jessica's death has finally surfaced."

That was an understatement. Josie would be devastated. Over the years she'd never given up hope. Josie had done everything she could to keep her child's disappearance in the public eye. She had been interviewed by the press and had made numerous appeals on the local news. She'd absolutely refused to believe that her child was dead.

"You worked the case?"

"Every gut-wrenching minute of it."

"Did anyone see what happened? Did witnesses come forward? Was there any DNA evidence or a sighting to help?" Ruth fired the questions at him.

He shook his head. "There was nothing. That's what made it so hard. I don't mean in terms of the work. We're all used to the hard slog. I'm talking about trying to rationalise what had happened. Kids don't just disappear, not in broad daylight with dozens of folk around. People see, they remember, and sooner or later they come forward. But not this time."

"The people you spoke to — reliable?"

He nodded. "One of the people present in the park that afternoon was Monika."

"Your Monika?"

"My *ex*, Monika. Ballsed that one up good and proper, didn't I? She wasn't even my Monika then." He heaved a sigh. "It was a lovely sunny day. Monika had gone to the park with a colleague. They'd taken a few of the residents from the care home. Monika was sitting on a bench, keeping tabs on them. She's an intelligent woman. She had her eyes and ears open, but even she saw nothing." Calladine thought for a moment, then came to a decision. "I'm going to ask her to walk me through it again. Do no harm."

"Jessica went missing from *Leesdon Park*?" Calladine nodded. "It'll have been busy. Summertime you say, school holidays. The place must have been chock-a-block with kids playing, and mums watching them."

"Yes, that's what people said at the time. What're you getting at?" He knew the tone. Ruth was in thinking mode. She had a shrewd, analytical mind and Calladine valued her input.

"If everything was as you describe, then someone must have seen something, stands to reason. But if not . . ."

"What are you trying to say?"

"Perhaps there was nothing to see."

Chapter 3

"I did think of that at the time, you know. I'm not entirely stupid. We looked into the possibility that Josie might have made the whole thing up," Calladine said.

Ruth looked at him. "And?"

"Although no one on the park could recall seeing anyone take the child, they did see Josie with the pushchair. The thing was bright pink. You could hardly miss it."

"But you did challenge Josie Wilkins's version of events?"

He nodded. "Yes, of course we did."

"And you thought her story was watertight?"

"At the time, yes. There were plenty of witnesses who saw her there with the pushchair."

"And now?"

In truth, Calladine was confused. His most abiding memory of the case was the relentless workload. That, and getting no results, whatever they tried. And they had tried everything. "I wasn't in charge of the investigation, remember. I was a mere sergeant back then."

"Hey! Thank you very much." She slapped his arm. "Believe me, there's nothing *mere* about being a sergeant."

Calladine managed a smile. "What did trouble me was Josie's fluctuating moods. On the day it happened she was exactly like you'd expect. A missing child. It's a parent's worst nightmare. In general, though, Josie Wilkins was something of a troublemaker. She drank, mostly in the pubs at the weekends. Once she'd gotten over the initial shock I expected more aggro from her, but there wasn't any."

"What do you mean?"

"After the initial shock, Josie became very subdued. Given her temperament, I expected fireworks. But she hardly seemed to be involved at all. She didn't ask about the exhaustive searches that we made. She didn't seem to be interested in the updates we gave her. She has an older sister, Tracy. Back then, Tracy lived with Josie and the child. She was definitely the dominant one. And as the investigation progressed, Tracy became more and more in control at the Wilkins home. But, looking back, I suppose she had to be. Josie was a mess. Given what had happened, and what she was like. I don't know why I expected anything else really."

"But she must have been in a state, surely?"

"Yes, she was. The day it happened she had to be hospitalised. She collapsed when she was being taken home from the station. Shock, the doctors said."

"Were both women upset about what had happened?" Ruth asked.

"Of course they were, but Tracy seemed more concerned with her sister's wellbeing than anything. She hardly let Josie out of her sight for weeks."

"Perhaps she was afraid that Josie might harm herself."

"Maybe, but thinking about it now, I reckon something else was going on."

"Like what?" Ruth asked.

"I don't know, and that's the problem. But looking at the case years later, I can see things more clearly. Stuff that didn't add up. Things that should have been of more concern to the team than they were."

Ruth looked at him. "What you're trying to say is that Josie's behaviour wasn't right."

"I'm not sure. It was right on the day the child disappeared. She gave a statement, told us all she could remember. But even then I thought she was holding something back. I tackled her about it and got a mouthful from Tracy for my trouble. To be honest, Josie was in no fit state. She must have been devastated. Apart from trying to take over, Tracy was a great help in many ways. She was a huge support to her sister. I doubt Josie would have made it through without her."

Calladine had gone over those few weeks many times. Given the absence of witnesses, evidence or sightings of the child, all he had been left was the family: their reactions and attitudes. And in Jessica's case, 'family' meant her mother, Josie, and Auntie Tracy. There were no other relatives, and no one, including Josie, knew who Jessica's father was. Tracy had told the investigation team that her sister had been seeing a number of men at that time. Most of them had been working on the construction of the new industrial estate on the outskirts of town. When the work was done, they moved on.

"But you did get Josie's side of the story. Who and what she recalled seeing the day the child was taken. If anyone had taken a particular interest in the little girl."

"After a fashion. Josie was in shock, so she was sedated for most of the time. Something else Tracy organised. I went round one morning to check on a couple of details, and Tracy had the GP there. As the weeks and months passed, Josie tried to get her act together. Eventually she did a couple of appeals on the local news and the radio. I think she got a taste for it. A piece was written about her in the paper. She campaigned for ages to keep the public aware of her plight. But none of it made any difference. No one came forward, so eventually she gave up."

"Back to the abduction. People saw Josie and the child at the park? What was she doing? Did she play with Jessica on any of the equipment, the swings? Did she talk to anyone, any of the other mothers?"

"No. Jessica was sleeping. Josie sat on a bench with the kid in her pushchair. She said she spent the time reading a magazine."

"Did any of the witnesses recall actually seeing Jessica, either awake or asleep?"

"People remembered all sorts of things. Josie, the pushchair, the fact that it was a nice day and very busy." Calladine thought for a few seconds. "I'll have to check the statements from the time, but no, I don't think anyone said anything about actually seeing the child for themselves. With it being sunny and Jessica being asleep, Josie had the hood up, and one of those sunshade things hanging over the front."

Ruth looked at him. "In that case you have to consider that the child might never have been there in the first place."

Calladine's stomach did that little flip thing which happened when he realised he'd missed something important. Why had no one picked up on that at the time? They'd all been blinded by the horror of a missing child. Taken in by the mother's shock. Calladine shook himself. This was stupid. The child had been with her mother in the park. It had happened like Josie said. Nothing else made any sense. Did it?

"Her reactions might have seemed a little strange as time went on," Calladine explained, "but that day Josie was genuinely shocked when she found her child gone. Her immediate reaction was what you'd expect. Witnesses were shocked too. We all thought her story had to be genuine. Subdued and cowed by her sister she might have become, but Josie was genuinely distraught that day. She wept buckets."

"If it's all the same, I'll keep an open mind for the time being."

When they reached the Duggan Centre car park, Calladine sat for a few minutes with the engine off. He sighed. "This isn't going to be easy either. How many times have we seen Julian since . . . well, since he came back to work?"

"All he wants is normal," Ruth reminded him. "He said so the last time we were here, don't you remember? No fuss, no soppy stuff. We had that chat."

It sounded fine the way Ruth put it. But now that they were here, how would it work in practice? "I can barely look at him," Calladine admitted. "Do you think he blames me?"

Ruth shook her head. "If he blames anyone, then it's got to be me. I was the one who took no notice of the information Nigel Hallam gave me. If I had . . ."

This was no good. They could blame themselves for what happened to Imogen, but it would get them nowhere. They had to at least make an effort. Julian Batho was the man they went to at times like this. He was the expert, and they needed him. Calladine turned to Ruth and gave her a half-hearted smile. "Who are we kidding? We both know who is really to blame for Imogen's murder."

"So stop beating yourself up. Donnelly is back behind bars, where he belongs."

Inside, the pair walked down the corridor towards Julian Batho's lab. They could see him through the glass-panelled wall, working. White coat on, head down, eyes glued to a slide under his microscope.

Calladine put on a smile. "Julian! Got something for you."

Julian looked up and regarded the pair for a few seconds. His expression didn't change. He looked miserable. Calladine consoled himself with the fact that

Julian invariably looked like that. He had a long face and irregular features. He didn't smile easily and rarely cracked a joke. Best just get on with it.

"This little lot was found bricked up behind a fireplace in Leesdon. I strongly suspect that the blanket and hairslide belonged to a child called Jessica Wilkins. You won't remember, it was before your time, but she disappeared about seventeen years ago. She wasn't quite two years old."

Julian took the ginger jar containing the ashes from Calladine's hands. He took the lid off and looked at them. "You think that these are her ashes?"

"Yes, I do."

Julian pointed. "These are in reasonable condition. Were they wrapped?"

"No. The ginger jar was wrapped in the blanket. Do you think you can get any DNA from the ashes?"

"If I find bone or teeth, yes, but it will take a while. I may get something from the blanket."

"We're going to see her mother next. If she's up to it, I plan to bring her in to look at these." Calladine pointed to the slide and blanket. "It's a tricky one. Much as I'd like to save her from the heartache, there's not a lot I can do."

Julian coughed and turned away. "Heartache is a fact of life, I'm afraid."

It was a reference to his own state of mind, had to be. Calladine ignored the comment. Dealing with Julian was difficult enough at the best of times. Currently it was way beyond him. "The house they were found in. We could do with a forensic team having a look."

"I agree. Leave the address and I'll organise it. Although what we'll be able to find after all these years is anybody's guess."

"Thanks, Julian." Calladine scribbled down the details for him.

"You okay?" Ruth asked.

Calladine caught her eye. Asking Julian that was a bit like lighting the blue touch paper.

But Julian was candid. "No, but I'm coping. I've put the house on the market. I've decided to go back into Leesdon centre. I'm moving into a flat in that block that overlooks the park."

Ruth nodded. "A fresh start."

"That, and the fact that I can't stand the house now that Imogen's not in it."

Ruth rubbed his arm. "You're not alone there. We feel a bit like that about the incident room. Rocco has done one. Got himself on a course in Wales just to be rid of the place."

"I'm hoping it'll get better," Julian admitted. "Feeling like this can't go on forever, surely?"

"Anytime you want to talk to us, Julian, just say. We all loved Imogen and we all miss her. We are the ones who know how you feel." She stood up on her toes and kissed his cheek.

Calladine felt a little envious. All this sympathy stuff, knowing what to say, it came so naturally to Ruth. She was warm, and people responded to her.

* * *

Natasha Barrington called out to Calladine and Ruth just as they were about to exit through the front door. "I'm planning on doing the PM on the girl first thing in the morning. I'd do it sooner but they're backing up in here, I'm afraid."

"We'll be there." Calladine gave a slight shudder. The idea of bodies backing up disturbed him. "Have you managed to estimate how long Flora had been dead?"

"At a guess, I'd say she'd been in the boot of that car for about a week. But it's tricky. The weather has been hot, and decomposition is advanced. Professor Batho is looking at the maggot life we found in the body. That will help us work things out."

"Anything on where she was killed?"

"We're doing a sweep of the immediate area. I'll keep you posted."

They made their way back to the car. "Poor kid," Ruth said. "Killed and stuffed in the boot of an old car. Folk have been walking past it all week. With the heat, you'd have thought someone would have smelled something. And I can't believe her mother didn't report her missing. A whole week! How old was she — sixteen or so? Flora's mum should have been banging on our door after a matter of hours."

Calladine nodded. "She wouldn't have been found even now if those kids hadn't been messing with the car. We'll have to speak to them later. Their statements don't make much sense. Too many contradictions. And we need to know a lot more about Flora's life and what she was up to. If her mother won't tell us, then we urgently need to find someone who will."

"Of course, the fact that Dolly Appleton did nothing about her missing daughter might mean she has something to hide," Ruth suggested.

"Or they'd had some almighty row," Calladine added. "It'll come out. We'll be speaking to her soon. Would you get Nigel to meet us at Heron House? It might be an idea to get a family liaison officer there too."

"It never stops in that place, does it? Bloody Hobfield. The place should be razed to the ground," Ruth said.

Chapter 4

The young man checked his reflection in the window of one of the flats. He stopped for a moment and straightened his tie. Smart, good-looking, he was a lifetime away from the scruffy kid that used to live here on the Hobfield. That incarnation of Ricky Hopwood was gone for good. In his place, had emerged a man with ambition, a man who would not be held back. A man who was going to make this hell-hole work for him.

Ricky was standing on the tenth deck of Heron House, outside number fifty. He banged on the door. "I know you're in, Mrs Appleton!" he shouted. "Make me wait any longer and next time it'll be my brother come knocking." That usually did the trick. People around here were terrified of getting a visit from Sean Hopwood. He liked to solve every problem with his fists. A little moronic for Ricky's taste, but it got results, and for that Sean had to be respected.

Ricky heard footsteps. She was standing behind the door, sobbing.

"I have nothing for you. Go away!" the woman shouted. Her voice cracked.

"Come on now, Mrs Appleton. This won't do. The debt is growing by the day. You need to show willing. Pay off something at least."

Suddenly the door was wrenched open. The woman facing him looked distraught. Her dark hair was dishevelled and her eyes were red and swollen from crying."

"My Flora is dead! Don't you know that? So bugger off and leave me alone. You can tell that bastard brother of yours to keep away too!"

"Whoa . . ." Ricky took several steps backwards. Word had travelled fast. The man in the newsagents had told Ricky. He was surprised the police weren't there. "I had nothing to do with your Flora," he said.

"You're a lying bastard! Both you and your brother. Most of what goes wrong around here has something to do with you two! If it's not you and Sean, it's you and them estate lads. You're always hanging around here making trouble."

"I'm sorry about your Flora, but the debt still needs paying. I had nothing to do with her death, so stick the blame elsewhere, Mrs Appleton. That's way out of order."

The look she gave him was poisonous. Her red eyes were full of hatred. "She was seeing one of you lot. She told me as much. She said the lad was taking her to a music festival, and that he'd paid for the tickets and everything. Do you know who that was?"

Ricky Hopwood shrugged. "I've no idea, Mrs Appleton, and you're wrong about me hanging out on the estate with the lads. I gave that up a long time ago."

"You're wasting your time here. I've got nothing for you." With that, Dolly Appleton slammed the door shut in his face.

Ricky Hopwood tutted and took his notebook from a suit pocket. He had no choice. Distasteful as it was, a visit from his brother was needed. Ricky left the rough stuff to him. The woman was way out of line. She deserved what was coming to her.

* * *

Calladine and Ruth got out of the lift just in time to hear the spat between Ricky and Dolly Appleton. They hurried along the tenth deck of Heron House towards the noise.

Calladine barred Ricky's way. "What's going on? We could hear you down on the ground floor."

Ricky shrugged. "Wasn't me. It was that woman shouting her head off. It was her throwing the foul language about. I'm just doing my job. It's not my fault if the punters won't pay up."

Calladine tried the door. It was locked. "Who're you chasing anyway?"

"Mrs Appleton. Payment's due today and she won't cough up."

Calladine wanted to grab the lad and shake him. Had he no compassion? "Dolly Appleton's daughter has just been found dead, for goodness' sake! The last thing she needs is a bloodsucking bastard like you on her back."

"Like I said, I've got a job to do."

"If I find you leaning on the people round here, I'll be on you like a ton of bricks." Calladine stepped closer to the young man and looked him straight in the eye. "Continue to prey on the vulnerable, and sooner or later, you and me are going to get serious."

Ricky Hopwood's smile was knowing. "You might be police but I've got the law on my side, copper. We are legal moneylenders. We have a licence, and we operate well within the guidelines. Try talking to this lot instead. Make them understand. They don't pay as agreed, we have no choice but to lean a little. It's either that or the bailiffs."

Ricky Hopwood walked off.

"Cheeky little—" Calladine spat.

"Moneylending?" Ruth pulled a face. "Bet they've got this place sewn up. The Hopwoods have been operating for years. Half of the estate owes them money."

Calladine shook his head. "First time I've seen Ricky since he was a kid. Now he's in cahoots with his big brother and I don't like it. It's a recipe for trouble."

"His brother? I haven't heard anything about Sean Hopwood in ages," Ruth said. "Sure he's still involved?"

"Oh, he's involved alright. Not being visible doesn't make him any less dangerous, just more careful. That one there," he nodded at the retreating figure of Ricky in his sharp suit, "is the acceptable face of their grubby little business. They need watching. Mark my words, it won't end well." He watched Ricky for a few moments. "Look at him! He's knocking on every door on the deck. Those loan sharks have certainly got the place under their thumb."

"Ruth! I thought it was you," a voice called out.

Calladine nudged her and nodded at the bloke walking along the deck towards them. He was tall, about the same age as Ruth and evidently in a hurry to speak to her.

"Glad I caught you. There's an outing you might be interested in. A rare bird alert in Shrewsbury."

Calladine was still watching Ricky Hopwood.

The man followed his gaze. "That's one of them Hopwoods. He's a bad 'un. It's in the blood, you know."

Ruth smiled at him. "We're keeping an eye out, Len."

"The trip's on Saturday — like I said, Shrewsbury. Frank's organising things with Annie. A night heron has taken up residence in a park there. It's roosting on a small island in the centre of a pool. Come if you want."

"Len is a member of our birding group," Ruth explained to Calladine.

"It must have got lost, or been blown off track. They are a rare visitor, if we get them at all. They're more usually found in Cyprus or Greece. Fascinating to watch, even for us old hands." Len sounded excited.

Ruth smiled at him. "I saw something about it on the telly. I wouldn't mind joining you."

"Just let Annie know. We're getting a minibus, need to know numbers. Who're you going to see?"

"Josie Wilkins," Ruth replied.

"Wish you well with that one. If she's not hiding from him," he nodded at Ricky Hopwood's disappearing back, "she'll most likely be off her head on the sofa." He walked off down the deck.

Calladine looked at Ruth. "Are you seriously thinking about going?"

"Might do. It'll make a change from spending the weekend shopping, cooking and seeing to Harry. Want to come?"

"God, no! Me and a bunch of twitchers?" Calladine shook his head.

"You might surprise yourself. They are an entertaining bunch, and there'll be a pub somewhere along the line."

Calladine wasn't to be persuaded. Instead, he said, "What did he mean, *off her head*?"

"Perhaps Josie has taken to drink, or worse, since she lost her child. I wouldn't blame her."

Calladine looked up and down the deck. Where was Nigel Hallam? "Let's get this over with. I'll have to speak to Josie. She'll have to be taken to the Duggan to identify the items. But I need to speak to Dolly Appleton too, as soon as."

Ruth nodded. "We'll do Josie first then. Give Dolly time to settle herself down after her run-in with Hopwood. I'll send Nigel a text, and tell him to wait outside for us. Once that's sorted, we'll move on to Dolly Appleton."

Josie Wilkins lived two floors up on the twelfth deck. The pair took the stairs. Calladine tapped lightly on the door.

He turned to Ruth. "We'll have to tread carefully. We can't say for sure that it's Jessica until we get the DNA. The first step is getting her to identify the hairslide and blanket." He tapped again. Josie was taking her time. They saw one of the curtains twitch and seconds later, she opened the door.

Calladine smiled at her. "Josie, how are you? It's been a while."

Josie stood in the doorway, and eyed them both with suspicion.

"This is a colleague of mine," said Calladine, "Sergeant Ruth Bayliss. Can we come in?"

Josie Wilkins's face had an indoor pallor. Her face was lined, and chiselled by grief into hard planes. Her dry, dyed-blonde hair had grey roots now, and although it was way past lunchtime, she was still wearing pyjamas and a dressing gown.

"I thought it was him prowling around, that Hopwood bloke. I've got nowt for him, so I didn't answer." She threw her fag end onto the deck and stood aside to let them in.

The three of them made the small sitting room look crowded.

"Something's happened," Calladine began.

"Jessica? Something to do with my Jess?" Her face lit up, and her eyes were suddenly bright. "You've found her? You know where she is?"

"It isn't good news, I'm afraid."

Josie Wilkins shrank before their eyes. Her eyes lost their lustre. She lowered herself slowly onto the sofa. "You've found her body?"

"We're not sure," said Ruth. "We've been given a jar containing some ashes. They may or may not be Jessica's. But two other items were also found. Those, coupled with the ashes, make us think there's a strong possibility that it's Jessica."

Calladine said simply, "They are a hairslide and a child's blanket."

"My Jess was wearing a slide in her hair," Josie said flatly. "You know the one, Inspector. So is it her or not? You've seen these things, so you must know."

Calladine didn't answer. He couldn't find the words. Josie stared up at him, her face full of suffering. All those years. Once again, he was about to wreck this woman's life and it unnerved him. He'd been to this flat many times when the case was active. Then, one day, after months of getting nowhere, he'd had to come and tell her the case was being wound down. Not shelved, it would always remain open, but they could no longer give it the same resources. Josie had blamed him. She'd flown at him, that day, fists flying. Called him all the names under the sun. Calladine had never been able to forget it. And now he was back. In many respects it was even worse this time. This time he had to tell her that there was nothing left to hope for. Her precious child was dead.

Ruth spoke for him. "They've gone to be analysed by our forensic people. We'd like to take you to have a look at them. The viewing won't take long and we'll bring you back home after."

"If these things are Jess's, what then?"

"We'll have the ashes tested, if that's possible. Forensics will try to extract some DNA. If they do, we'll match it with yours. Then we'll know for sure."

Ruth had explained it so simply. Calladine felt as if he'd been struck dumb. What was wrong with him?

Josie Wilkins suddenly realised what the ashes meant. "Someone burned her?" She jumped to her feet, and began to walk to and fro across the room. "Who could do such a thing? She was only a baby, tiny for her age. You have to find out. I need to know what happened."

"Let forensics do their bit first, then we'll try to make sense of things."

All at once, Josie burst into tears. "I want Tracy! She'll have to come with me. I can't do this on my own."

Chapter 5

Calladine left Ruth with Josie while he went to speak to Dolly Appleton. Ruth would ring him when Tracy turned up. With a heavy heart, he walked back down the stairs, along the deck and rang the bell. He hated this part of the job, always had. He looked around, but there was still no sign of Nigel Hallam.

"Who is it?" Dolly called from behind the door.

"Police, Mrs Appleton. I need a word." He heard a key turn in the lock, and a bolt slide back. The likes of Ricky Hopwood had a lot to answer for.

Dolly Appleton stared at him. Her eyes were swollen from crying and her face was haggard and gaunt from lack of sleep. She looked dreadful.

"That body. It's her, isn't it? It is my Flora you've found? It's all over the estate. You should have come and told me sooner." Her voice shook, whether from anger or sorrow, it was hard to tell.

Calladine nodded. "I'm sorry. I had to wait until we were absolutely sure. She hadn't been reported missing, you see. However, this morning dental records confirmed that it was Flora. Can I come in, have a chat? I won't keep you long."

Dolly moved aside to let him in. "I knew it. I've felt something was wrong all week. But I don't understand what she was doing in the boot of that car! Apart from that, no one has told me anything. I don't know what you think I can tell you."

They went into a small sitting room, a replica of Josie Wilkins's.

"Let's start with the last time you saw Flora," said Calladine.

"I haven't seen her for more than a week. A week last Friday, to be exact." There were fresh tears in her eyes.

"Perhaps you can tell me why she left home, and why you didn't report her missing."

She sighed. "I'm going to regret that for the rest of my days. The truth is, that night she disappeared we'd had a row. Flora was in a rotten mood, she had been all day. She had a thing for this boy, and he'd let her down. They were planning to go to a music festival together. It had been booked and paid for weeks ago. Then they had an argument, and he finished it. That night, the last time I saw her, she was determined to go and have it out with him. I tried to reason with her. I asked her to stay in, to calm down, but she wouldn't listen."

"Who was this boy?"

"She wouldn't tell me. All I know is that he's local and probably older than her. Flora was angry. She got all dressed up, wore her leather jacket, put on make-up and did her hair. Flora could look a lot older than sixteen at times." Dolly frowned. "She was going to that pub, the Pheasant, on the edge of the estate. I told her not to. There's always trouble there, and I didn't want her getting mixed up in any."

"Flora was underage. Had she been there before?"

"I think so. She knew the landlord. Like I said, she could look a lot older. I did try, really I did, but she wouldn't listen. Headstrong was Flora, did as she pleased."

"So when she didn't come home, what did you do?"

"I went round the next morning. I spoke to the landlord but he said Flora hadn't been there at all. He knows her, and apparently the pub hadn't been busy, so he would have noticed. I was worried. I was about to report her missing, but then I got the text."

This was news to Calladine. "Text? Show me."

Dolly took her mobile from the table and scrolled through her calls and texts. "Here it is." She handed it to him.

'Don't worry, mum, I'm fine. I'm going to that festival with a mate. Cheer myself up. I'll be back mid-week xx.'

Calladine looked at her. "Was this normal behaviour for Flora? Had she taken off on her own before? She was only sixteen."

"She went to a festival last year with a couple of her friends. Flora was a sensible girl. She knew how to handle herself. There has only ever been me and her."

Nonetheless, Calladine thought, sixteen was a bit young to be allowed to wander off at will for days on end. "Where was this festival held?"

"North Yorkshire, near Knaresborough."

"Mrs Appleton, did you hear from Flora again after this text?" Dolly's eyes searched the room as if looking for the answer there. Then she shook her head.

"I tried ringing her. I texted her back, umpteen times, but got nothing. I put it down to the signal being bad."

Flora had been dead for a week, so she'd probably never left the Hobfield. Calladine couldn't explain this to her mother until he had the PM and forensic reports to confirm it. "Tell me about her friends. Who was she closest to?"

"Her best friend was Isla Prentice. They've been close since they started school together at five years old." She paused, and bit on her bottom lip. "But I don't think they've been getting on so well of late. I suspect they'd argued about that boy Flora liked."

"Where does Isla live?" he asked.

"Circle Road, number eleven."

Calladine made a note of the address. He gave Dolly his card. "Do you have someone who can come sit with you?"

She shook her head. "I'll ring my sister. She'll come, but she lives in Newcastle."

"I'll send a female PC to sit with you for a while. If there's anything you want, or if you recall anything else, you can tell her. She'll pass the information on."

Dolly nodded. Calladine decided to wait for more information before he spoke to her again.

Ruth was waiting outside with Nigel.

Calladine nodded at the DC. "I want you to find the three lads that found the body, and take them down to the station. Their names and addresses are on the statements. Ring Joyce, she'll text you the info. They were holding something back last night. All three of them were very cagey. Keep it light, and make sure they know that they are not in any trouble. Organise a uniform to go with you. We need to have a word with the landlord of the Pheasant."

* * *

Calladine and Ruth returned to Josie's flat and waited outside. Calladine looked at his watch. "What's she up to?"

"She wanted to get dressed," Ruth said, "so I left her to it. I also think she wanted to talk to Tracy when she turns up."

Calladine shook his head. "Let's hope we can get it over with quickly. Josie often becomes confused, what with the drink and goodness knows what else she takes. Tracy is the sorted one. She's got a lot of influence with Josie. She's been looking after her all her life. Even when they were kids, Tracy took charge. Their mother wasn't up to much, as I recall."

"Where does Tracy live?"

"One floor up. After what happened, she decided to stay near her sister. She's okay. Works for Leesworth Council. It's a good job, and I'm sure she could afford to live somewhere better, but she won't leave her Josie."

"Married?" asked Ruth.

"No."

"Children?"

"No. Seeing to Josie must have put paid to a lot of things in Tracy's life."

Ruth's mouth turned down. "How was the Appleton woman?"

"Devastated, as you would expect. Turns out she thought Flora had gone to a music festival. And she had a boyfriend, although Dolly doesn't know who he was. We'll talk to the best friend later. Hopefully we'll glean more from her."

The minutes passed. Calladine paced up and down with his hands in his pockets. He knew the Jessica Wilkins case inside out. There had been no mention of any Beardsell Terrace, so why had her remains ended up there? He made a mental note to look for a connection with any names in the file as soon as he got back to the nick. The idea of finding something they'd missed at the time terrified him. He racked his brain. He was certain nothing had slipped through the net, nothing important anyway. He'd been there. They'd done everything, gone over every scrap of evidence several times. Anyone of any interest had been thoroughly checked out.

Calladine would never be able to forgive himself if they'd overlooked something vital. The idea made him feel sick. He'd lived through Josie's horror, every second of it. He'd seen the look on her face today. The glimmer of hope smashed to bits when Ruth told her what had been found. This visit to the Duggan wasn't going to be easy.

"If this is right, if you have found Jess, she won't cope." Tracy Wilkins strode towards them. She was a tall, slim woman with dark hair that bobbed on her shoulders and framed her elfin face. "I'm telling you now, it'll finish her."

Calladine gave her a weak smile. "Thanks for helping, Tracy."

"I'm not doing this for you. This is for Josie. She's delicate, needs careful handling. I just hope this isn't some wild goose chase." She gave Calladine a warning look.

He inhaled. "I don't think it is. Only forensic tests will give us the definitive answer, but I think what we've got is the real thing."

Tracy pushed past him and went into the flat.

Ruth studied the closed door. "Knows her own mind, that one."

"Always has, Ruth. Tracy was the sensible one."

"Josie is in her late thirties. How old is her sister?" Ruth asked.

Calladine shrugged. "I'm not certain, but I reckon she's a couple of years older."

The door remained closed. "Very alike, aren't they?"

"Except that Tracy has taken care of herself. She holds down a responsible job. After what happened, Josie went into a downward spiral that she's never escaped from."

"I can understand that." Ruth shuddered. "I don't know what I'd do if anything happened to Harry. I can't imagine how people live after stuff like that. The horror of wondering what might have happened to your child. How they died, what was done to them. It'd kill me."

After another few minutes, the two women appeared in the doorway. Josie Wilkins was in jeans, battered trainers and a sweatshirt that had seen better days. Her arms were folded against her body, as if to hold herself together. In contrast, Tracy was dressed in a skirt and a smart jacket. She'd obviously come from work. As Ruth had noted, the two women were alike, but the trauma of losing Jessica had ravaged Josie's looks. She didn't seem to give a damn what she looked like. Tracy, on the other hand, evidently took pride in her appearance.

Ruth nudged his arm. "We should get going."

* * *

Josie Wilkins clung to her sister's arm. Head down, she shuffled along the corridor to the room where Professor Julian Batho was waiting for them. Ruth led the way, with Calladine following in their wake.

Tracy patted her hand. "You'll be okay, Josie. Take your time. I'm with you."

Ruth opened the door and stood aside for the two women. She and Calladine followed them into the room. The little pink blanket and hairslide lay on a table — small, insignificant items that had the power to tear apart what was left of Josie's tattered life.

She gasped. Her hands flew to her face and she cried out. She reached forward, picked up the blanket and held it to her chest, weeping. In silence they watched her caress the appliqued gold teddy bear.

"It's Jess's!" she howled. "I'd know it anywhere."

Julian coughed. "It has been a long time. You are quite sure?"

Josie Wilkins regarded him with cold eyes. "You have never raised an infant or you wouldn't ask that. You have no idea how important a small piece of fabric like this could be to a child. It's a comfort thing. My Jess wouldn't go to sleep without it."

Calladine moved forward to stand beside her. "And the slide? What do you think?"

"Yes! Yes! They both belonged to Jessica." She looked at Calladine. "I want to see her!"

Julian shook his head. "I'm sorry, but that is not possible."

"She's my child! I insist on it! I have the right."

Tracy Wilkins looked at them, and then took her sister's arm. "They are not being unkind, sis. There is nothing to see, really. Ashes, you said when you phoned me. You don't want to see that. It'll stay with you forever."

Josie was screaming now. "What will happen to her? My baby! I want to stay near my baby!"

Julian looked at Calladine and Ruth. "I'll organise some tea."

Calladine nodded. Julian was floundering. All he'd be wanting now was to get out of that room.

"You can wait next door," Julian told them. "I'll arrange for some tea to be brought through."

"When will I know if the ashes are really hers?" Josie asked. She seemed a little calmer now.

Calladine looked at her. "It will take a while. The tests are not as simple as with . . ." He'd been about to say blood or tissue, but swallowed his words.

"You will be reopening the investigation, Inspector?" asked Tracy.

"Depending on what the DNA throws up. But since Josie has positively identified the two items, we will do a thorough search of the place where they were found."

Tracy looked at him. "Where was that?"

"I can't say," said Calladine.

"Local?"

Calladine turned away, avoiding her penetrating gaze. "Here's the tea."

* * *

Josie rode home in a daze. Everything had happened so fast, and so completely out of the blue. Had they really found her Jess? She could hardly believe it. Her head was in a whirl, her mind filled with images and half-understood conversations from that time. There was such a lot she couldn't work out.

"He was right, that copper. The truth needs to be told." Josie looked at her sister, tears in her eyes. "This has brought it all back. I keep seeing things, hearing words in my head, people shouting." She sighed heavily. "You should have told them what really happened."

The look her sister gave her was chilling. "If we were going to do that, we should have done it seventeen years ago. We can't say anything now. It'd be us behind bars for withholding evidence."

Josie shook her head. "It was you that clammed up. Besides, what evidence? I still don't understand. What didn't we tell them? I keep getting flashbacks, but none of it makes any sense."

"You were off your head on smack and booze. What do you expect?"

Josie started to sob. "I lost my little girl, and I can't remember how. But then I start to think that I didn't lose her at all. That it wasn't my fault. I remember other things too, strange things, stuff that doesn't add up." She stared at her sister with anxious eyes. "Sometimes I think I wasn't even *in* the bloody park that afternoon."

"Now you're being stupid. Of course you were. You're upset. You have a rest, and then everything will seem clearer."

"You would tell me, wouldn't you, Trace, if there was something else? When I think back to that day, all I remember is shouting, people drunk in my flat. I don't know what was real and what wasn't."

"There you are then. You were ill. You'd had a lot of treatment for drug addiction. You were taking pills and the like. Your head was a mess back then, Josie. Accept it and stop stressing."

Chapter 6

It was late afternoon when Calladine and Ruth returned to the station. The first thing they heard was laughter. Nigel Hallam had left the three lads unattended in a small anteroom. Calladine knew from their statements that they were all over eighteen. They should know better than to behave like little kids.

Heaving a sigh of frustration, Calladine stuck his head around the door. "Keep it down," he ordered sharply.

One of them called back, "I'm done here. We've been hanging around this dump for ages."

The voice belonged to Kyle Logan. Calladine knew the lad by reputation. He'd been in trouble a couple of times for fighting, but so far had managed to get off with warnings. From the look of him, he'd learned nothing. He had a black eye, which had faded to a lurid shade of yellow. He lived with his father, Bernie. Bernie Logan was a waster who spent most of his time and money in the local betting shop.

"Believe me, lads, I'm not in the mood. You'll be in and out of here just as soon as we get to the truth."

Calladine turned to Ruth. "Bring me the statements from the office."

"I've got work soon," Kyle shouted. "And if I'm late, there'll be hell to pay. Mark's got a short fuse." He rubbed his injured eye.

"Did he give you that?" Calladine asked.

"It was an accident. I knocked it with a pan at work, it's nothing serious."

Calladine doubted that was the truth. But if the lad wouldn't make a complaint, there was nothing he could do. For now, he needed to check their statements. "I want the truth about when you found Flora last night. I want to know where you'd all been, and if anyone else was with you."

Dean Roberts gave him a shifty, sideways glance. "That other copper wrote it all down. We wasn't telling lies, and we didn't hurt Flora neither. You can't pin anything on us."

Calladine sat down and smiled at them. "That's not what this is about. You are here because there are inconsistences in your statements. So we'll go over the events again. You can start by telling me where you met up last night."

The three lads looked at one another. Jack Cope shrugged. "We were hanging out around the estate."

"It was a dreadful night. Can't have been much fun." Calladine looked from one to the other. "You must have met up for a reason."

No response.

"So what took you across the estate to that car?"

Ruth returned with the statements. Calladine took them and gestured for her to sit down. "Kyle, it says here that you called for Dean, and then you wandered around the estate until you *happened* across the car."

Kyle Logan fidgeted on his seat, his eyes fixed on the floor.

Again it was Jack who spoke. "It was me and Dean that met up first."

After a few seconds, Kyle added, "Got mixed up, didn't I? I mean, we'd just found a dead 'un in the boot. I wasn't thinking straight."

"Where were you, Kyle? How did the others *happen* across you?"

He frowned. "I'd just finished my shift at the Pheasant. The car was only a stone's throw away. It had been there for ages. I know for a fact that Marshal leaves it unlocked and the key under the seat. We fancied a ride, that's all."

Calladine looked sternly at them. "That's theft."

"Marshal wouldn't have been bothered. He wants it gone. Got no money for repairs or insurance."

"So who was going for this ride?"

"Me, Jack, Dean. And the girl."

Calladine scanned the statements again. "There is no mention of a girl in any of your statements. Who is she, Kyle?"

"Isla Prentice," he replied. "She was Flora's bestie. She was with us because her and Flora had fallen out, and she has a thing for Ricky."

"Ricky Hopwood? There's no mention of him either."

Dean sat forward. "He wasn't with us. Isla's wasting her time mooning after him. Ricky couldn't give a stuff about her. He'd no intention of meeting up. Besides, he was still working."

"So why did you leave her out?" Calladine waved the statements in their faces. "All of you."

"Like I said, we was all in shock," Kyle mumbled.

"We didn't think it mattered," Dean added. "She didn't do anything or touch the car. She was just there. She complained about the smell."

"She wasn't there when the police turned up either. There was just the three of you."

"She felt sick. So we said she should go home," Jack said.

Calladine had a sneaking suspicion that something else was going on here. He decided to leave it for now. "So tell me what led up to you finding Flora."

"We were going to take Isla for a run, but she kept going on about the smell," Dean told him. "It was disgusting. But Marshal is a mucky sod. He could have left anything rotting away inside that car."

"Which one of you opened the boot?"

"That was me," admitted Jack.

Calladine grimaced, a sympathetic look. "That can't have been pleasant."

Jack shook his head. "It was bloody awful. The body — Flora — was stuffed in there like rubbish. Her skin looked black and it was falling off. She was covered in blood and flies. I couldn't take it in. *He* threw up." He grinned and nodded towards Dean. "Isla kept jumping around, waving her arms at the flies. When she saw what was in the boot, she lost it. Started screeching and carrying on. We had to let her go home."

Ruth interjected, "Was Flora friendly with you lot? Did she used to hang around with you?"

"Nah, she was too busy down the Pheasant."

Calladine looked at them. The Pheasant kept coming up in this enquiry. "Why that pub? What was the attraction?"

The lads looked at each other again. No one said anything.

"It was Ricky," Kyle said at last. "That's where he goes."

Calladine made a note of this. "Quite the ladies' man is our Ricky, isn't he? Were they seeing each other?"

Kyle shrugged. "Dunno. He can be dead secretive sometimes, can Ricky."

Chapter 7

Back in the incident room Calladine gave the amended statements to Joyce, to put in the case file, and then updated the incident board. "We need to speak to Ken Marshal, Isla Prentice, and Wallace — the landlord of the Pheasant." He counted them off on his fingers. "We'll see Isla first. She lives on Circle Road."

Nigel Hallam was not at his desk. Calladine turned to Joyce. "Has Nigel made any headway on finding out who used to live at Beardsell Terrace?"

Joyce shrugged. "He was doing some research earlier but he didn't say if he'd got anything."

"Did he say where he was going?" asked Calladine.

"He says very little to me. He grabbed his notes about an hour ago and went out."

Calladine was all for his team using their own initiative, but it was usual for them to leave word about what they were up to. "If he comes back, get him to ring me."

"Would you see what you can find out about the Prentice family and text me?" Ruth asked Joyce. "It might help to have some background."

* * *

Circle Road ran three quarters of the way around the outside of the Hobfield Estate. The houses were in neat blocks of six with small front gardens. Most of them looked out towards the tower blocks, but some were lucky enough to have a view over the common and the hills beyond.

The Prentice home was one of these. It looked well-kept. The square of lawn was freshly mown, with a flower border running round it.

Ruth read from the text Joyce had sent her. "Isla lives with her mother. The father is dead, apparently. The mother works for Leesworth Council."

"Same as Tracy Wilkins," Calladine remarked. "Wonder if they know each other?"

Ruth sighed. "One case at a time, please, Tom. We're pushed enough as it is. Rocco is away and Nigel Hallam is off the boil. I think something is bothering him. Has he said anything to you?"

Calladine shook his head. Ruth was right about Nigel — and the workload. Nothing was happening with the Jessica Wilkins case at the moment, but that was only until Julian came up with his findings. Then they would be rushed off their feet.

"Let's get these done and dusted, then we can call it a day."

Isla herself answered the door. She was a pretty girl, pale with auburn hair. She stared at them, and her face flushed red when they showed her their badges. Ruth gave her a smile. "Is your mum in? We'd like a word about last night."

"She's doing tea." Isla stood aside to let them in. "Was it . . . Flora in that car?" Her voice shook. "People are saying it was. They're saying she's been murdered. It was awful. I've never seen a dead body before."

"Yes, it was your friend," Ruth replied gently. "But we don't know what happened to her yet."

Isla's mum, Joan Prentice, emerged from the kitchen. She was a tall woman and thin. She had very short hair which did her long face no favours. She nodded towards the sitting room. "We'll sit in here."

They all sat down, Joan and Isla on the edge of their chairs. Joan looked from Calladine to Ruth. "This has really upset Isla and no mistake. I don't know what she can tell you."

Calladine turned to the girl. "Well, for starters, can you tell me who you were with last night?"

"Kyle, Dean and Jack." She shrugged her thin shoulders. "Ricky was supposed to be there too, but he couldn't make it."

"Ricky Hopwood?" Ruth compressed her lips. "He's quite a bit older than you, isn't he, Isla?"

"I don't care." She gave her mother a defiant look. "He went out with Flora, and she was my age. They were close for months. I know he likes me. He and Flora were having problems anyway."

Mrs Prentice shook her head. "Don't for one second think that I approve. The boy's a bad 'un. That brother of his is a rogue, and Ricky's no better."

"When did you last see Flora?" Calladine asked.

Mrs Prentice answered. "Flora was here on the Friday. The pair of them were upstairs in Isla's bedroom until late. That damn festival was on Saturday, and she was trying to persuade Isla to go with her. But I had put my foot down. In my opinion they were both too young."

"I thought Flora was going with a boy," Ruth chipped in. "That he'd booked and paid for the event."

Isla nodded. "Ricky."

"Are you sure?" asked Calladine.

"They had been seeing each other but like I said, he'd lost interest. At the last minute he pulled out. He was telling anyone who'd listen that he was sick of her. She was too possessive, and he wanted rid."

Ruth looked at her. "So you didn't go with her?"

Mrs Prentice interjected. "There was no way I'd let her! An event like that is no place for two sixteen-year-olds on their own. Flora came and went as she pleased. Her mother never did have any control."

"Did you and Flora argue about the festival?" asked Calladine.

Isla nodded. "Flora had a spare ticket. She said I could have it for nowt. She said I was soft for doing what my mum wanted. Anyway, I told her there was no way, and she left."

"Do you know where she went when she left here?"

Isla had her eyes on her hands, fiddling with the rings on her fingers. "She told me she had plans, but nothing else."

Calladine guessed that she was hiding something. "You won't get into trouble for telling me what you know."

She was silent for a moment, then glanced up, quickly. "Flora said she was going to that pub. She thought Ricky would be there."

Calladine tried to catch her eye. "When the police arrived at the car on Friday night you had already left. Why was that? Why didn't you stay with the others?"

Isla's mother spoke for her. "Came home in a right state, she did, and it wasn't the first time either. Told me she'd had a row with some girls and went straight up to her room. It was those girls who set on you the week before, wasn't it, Isla? Why don't you tell the detectives about them? Perhaps they can have a word, make them stop."

Isla rounded on her mother. "I'm fine!" She turned to Calladine. "I was in shock on Friday. I couldn't take in what we'd found."

"Go on, Isla." Calladine leaned towards her.

"I was scared. I didn't feel up to answering all the questions. I knew my mum would find out that I'd been hanging out with those lads and she'd be angry. But they're alright really. I enjoyed hanging out with them. Flora and the lads were fun to be with, a right laugh."

Mrs Prentice interrupted again. "She needs to stay away. They're a bad lot, all of them."

"Okay, that'll do for now. But we will need to speak to you again." Calladine handed Mrs Prentice a card. "If Isla recalls anything else that might help, then ring me."

* * *

When they were back in the car, Ruth asked, "What did you think?"

"I'm wondering what they are all hiding. Those lads were holding back about something Isla did when they found Flora. She wasn't around when uniform turned up. Now Isla herself is being cagey about Flora's movements. I think Isla Prentice knows a lot more than she's saying."

"We could do with having a word with Ricky Hopwood, couldn't we?" Ruth said.

Calladine nodded. "We will, and we'll speak to that lot again. But first we should see Marshal, and speak to the landlord of that pub. We'll leave Ricky until we see what the PM throws up."

* * *

Ken Marshal lived in a ground-floor flat in Fieldfare House. Calladine banged on the door but got no response. "We'll have to come back tomorrow."

A voice rang out from a neighbouring flat. "He's gone to stay with his sister, love."

Calladine peered around. "Do you know when he'll be back?"

"Couple of days tops. He can't stand her husband."

Calladine made a note. They'd have to return later in the week.

Ruth indicated a patch of rutted, oily concrete a few feet from the building. "That's where he left the car. The pub is only just across there." She nodded at the dilapidated building. A sign reading, 'Th- P-easant,' creaked slowly in the wind. "No distance at all."

The two of them walked over and went in. It was gone six in the evening, but the pub was empty.

"Wonder how popular this place is?" Calladine nodded towards the specials board on the wall. "They do food."

"Kyle Logan works here, so it must do some trade to afford his wages."

A big, burly man called to them from behind the bar. "You're police, aren't you? Well, you're wasting your time. That girl hasn't been in here for ages. So I can't help." He folded his thick arms.

Calladine smiled at him, and flashed his badge. "News travels fast round here. We've just a few questions and then we'll leave you in peace, Mr Wallace."

Calladine noted the wary look and the nervous glances towards the door that led into the kitchen. "I took this place over three months ago. I'm trying to turn it round, but few folk round 'ere have cash to spend. Still, it's not doing too badly. The food helps keep the tills ringing. I don't want you lot frightening away what clients I do have."

Calladine smiled again. "A couple of questions then we'll be out of your hair. We're interested in knowing when Flora Appleton was last in here."

Wallace coughed. "She's underage for a start. I've had to tell her any number of times, and that young man of hers."

"Ricky Hopwood?" Ruth asked.

"That's him. But I can't come down too hard because he's one of the few around here who occasionally has money in his pocket."

"Only occasionally? The Hopwoods are loaded, surely?" Odd thing to say, thought Calladine. The Hopwoods were coining it in. It had to mean that Sean kept Ricky short, but why?

"All I know is what I see. Most nights Ricky's got empty pockets."

Calladine asked him again. "When did you last see Flora, Mr Wallace?"

He shrugged. "Wednesday or Thursday, before she did one on the Saturday."

"Not the Friday night? She didn't come in looking for Ricky?" asked Calladine.

Wallace shook his head.

"How about Ken Marshal? Have you seen him?"

Wallace coughed again. "No. Bit of a loner that one."

"Okay, that'll do for now. We'll talk again."

They turned and left, to Wallace's obvious relief.

Outside, Calladine put his hand to his head, exasperated. "Another reluctant witness. What is it with folk around here?"

Ruth shrugged.

"There must be something dodgy going on. Wallace, Kyle and Ricky Hopwood could all be involved. Doesn't help the case though, does it?"

"Okay. I'll take you back to the nick and we'll knock off. It's getting on. Will Jake have picked Harry up from nursery?"

"If he hasn't, Tom, I'll kill him. I don't ask much. I mean, it's on his way home. It's the least he can do."

Ruth and Jake's problems bothered Calladine. He wanted Ruth to be happy. He'd encouraged her relationship with Jake. If they did split up it would hit her hard. Ruth might make with the brave words, but he knew very well that this was grinding her down.

Calladine decided to update the board in the morning. He left Ruth in the car park and headed home. It didn't take him long. He turned onto the High Street, then cut through the back roads. Next to his stone terraced house, a large white van was parked with its wheels half on the kerb. The house next door had been up for rent. Someone must be moving in.

As soon as he got out of his car, a woman called out to him. "Hello! You must be my new neighbour. Or I'm yours — take your pick." She walked towards him, wearing a big smile.

Calladine put her at about forty. She was a little shorter than him with long deep-chestnut hair, with those highlights that Ruth liked so much. The lights from the van made them shine like gold.

She held out her hand. "Layla Calvert. You?"

"Tom Calladine." He gently shook her manicured hand.

Another big smile revealed perfect teeth. "The woman over the road said you were a policeman."

He nodded. "I am. I'm a detective inspector with Leesdon CID."

She looked impressed. "We can all feel safe in our beds in that case. Is that your dog?"

On seeing Calladine, Sam had started to bark. He was now peering at them from the front room window. Calladine fished the house keys from his pocket. "He wants his tea."

"Nice dog. Does he stay in all day on his own?" she asked with concern.

"No, the lady next door takes him out and spends some time with him. They're great pals." Calladine smiled.

"I'll see you around, then." She gave him a grin and went back to the van.

Chapter 8

"What d'you call this?" Sean Hopwood was counting the cash from his brother's money bag, and he was angry. "Heron House alone should have brought in three grand." Ricky was going about this all wrong. At this rate they'd be out of business within the month. "You're a waste of bloody space!" He lashed out with his fist, catching Ricky's cheek.

Ricky fell backwards onto the floor. He sat up and rubbed his face. "That's twice this week you've landed me one. You need to rein in that temper of yours or you'll do me some real damage!"

"And *you* need to wake up. If you don't, there'll be a whole lot more where that came from. Idiot! You've let them walk all over you." Sean threw the cloth bag onto the table, and looked his brother up and down. "You need to toughen up, sunshine. A bruise or two will do you good. You're far too smart-looking for starters. Them women will think you're a poofter."

Ricky rubbed his face. "There was no need for that! I do my best, you know."

"No, you don't. You ponce up and down them decks, smiling, drinking their tea. It's not what's needed. You have to force them to pay up, even if it takes a bit of unfriendly persuasion." Sean Hopwood's sneer revealed a mouthful of rotting teeth. He eyed the bruise that was rapidly developing on his brother's face. "Where do you think the money comes from to buy those fancy clothes? Like I said, you need to be more careful. Give me the book. I'll pay one or two of the punters a little visit and I won't be so damned agreeable. I give a couple of these a slap or two and word will soon get round."

"Some copper was nosing about. He warned me off. Threatened to get shirty if I leant on the punters too hard."

"The law can't touch us, Ricky boy. Remember, we're legit. I've told you, those people need us."

Ricky was at the mirror again, pawing at his cheek.

Sean had had enough. "Give over! You should try giving the business as much attention as you give that pretty face of yours. Like having a roof over your head, do you? Because if you don't shape up, this fancy house will have to go." Sean was sick and tired of carrying Ricky. He'd been doing it all his life. The boy couldn't do a thing right. It had always been that way, and he was worn out with covering his back.

"That girl," said Ricky, "Flora Appleton. She's been found dead, murdered so they are saying. Her mum was cut up, shouting abuse, and blaming everyone for what happened, including me."

Sean stared at his brother. "She's wrong though, isn't she? Tell me you weren't involved in that girl's death."

Ricky's face reddened. "I wasn't! I liked Flora. I wouldn't hurt her."

"Is that why the mother didn't pay up?" Sean grabbed the book and checked against her name. "Nothing! Neither that bitch nor that waster that calls himself Kyle's father have offered a bean." Sean Hopwood was seething.

His younger brother was too dumb to realise when he was being taken for an idiot. "That killing had nowt to do with us. Her mother is using it to duck out of paying what she owes. That won't wash with me. She'll be first on the list for later."

"Mrs Appleton is distraught. She's far too upset and angry about what happened to bother with me. Can't say I blame her either. It must be dreadful to lose someone like that. I'm going to miss her too. Me and Flora spent a lot of time together. We might even have got serious given half a chance. What if the woman goes to the police? Tells them we're hassling her? They will ask me some awkward questions."

"*Mrs Appleton!* Listen to yourself! You sound like you're selling insurance. You're a debt collector, kid. You have to be hard. At the first sign of softness the bastards will walk all over you. Forget the girl! She's bought it, hasn't she? Nowt to do with you, so don't get involved."

The boy just didn't have the right stuff. Sean had tried to toughen him up, but Ricky hadn't learnt a thing. "You go on that estate to do your job, and that's it. I've told you, the more you bring in, the more I pay you. Don't collect, don't earn. Simple as that. I don't want you hanging around with that idiot Kyle and his mates either. Or with some random girl. That Kyle is no good for you or anyone else. All he does is dish out blow and booze." Ricky was still fussing with his face. Sean Hopwood sighed. "You need to get real, kid. This is a business. They don't pay, we don't eat."

"I've been mates with Kyle since school."

"Well, you're not mates anymore. And less of the back-chat! You do as you're told!"

"What are you going to do about the non-payers? You won't hurt anyone too much, will you? The police are all over the Hobfield because of the murder. We will get into bother if you are heavy-handed with the punters."

Sean's eyes narrowed. "I'll do whatever I want. No one will tell on us, boy. They know better than to grass up Sean Hopwood."

* * *

Sean Hopwood waited until it was dark before going in search of Bernie Logan. He knew Bernie's habits of old. He would spend all day in the Pheasant getting tanked up, and then he'd stagger home. Well, if he had money for booze, he could sodding well pay his debts.

Sean waited in the alley that ran along the side of Heron House. He was prepared to hang around all night if necessary, but he was in luck. Logan returned just before nine. Now for that much-needed lesson.

The first punch came at Bernie out of nowhere. "Bastard! Let go of me!" he screamed. He tried to defend himself, flailing his fists about, trying to connect with Sean's face. But he was too drunk. It was impossible to fight back when he couldn't even walk straight.

Sean grabbed him by the scruff of his neck, pulling his head back. Then he let go, allowing Bernie to fall forward. Bernie fell face down on the ground, winded. Sean rolled him over.

He jabbed his finger into Bernie's chest. "First, I want my money. Then I want you to tell that scroat of a son of yours to lay off bothering our Ricky. I don't want to hear that they've been hanging out together. Got it?"

"I've got no money!" Bernie protested with a groan. "I'm not working and Kyle earns a pittance."

"You've got money to buy booze in that pub. Where does that come from?"

"Kyle makes a little, here and there. He keeps me sorted."

"He's still dealing around the estate. He's been seen, people talk. If I see you or him anywhere near Ricky, I'll tear your bloody heads off."

"I've got nowt left," Bernie insisted. "Check, see for yourself. Me pockets are empty."

Sean had heard enough excuses from this lot to last him a lifetime. He smashed his fist into Bernie's face. Blood poured from Bernie's nose. He cried out, but now Sean was beside himself. He couldn't stop. He rained down blow after blow, thick and fast. Finally he stood up, breathing heavily, but he hadn't finished yet. A hefty kick to Bernie's kidneys made him scream in agony. He coughed and rolled into a tight ball. Sean landed several more savage kicks, then one last brutal stamp on Bernie's head. Bernie lay still.

Leaving Bernie, Sean took the lift up to the tenth floor. He was out of condition and his heart pounded. Impelled by rage and adrenalin, he was in no mood to listen to another whining sob story. He hammered on Dolly Appleton's door until his fist hurt. "Open up, bitch, or I'll kick the bugger in!"

He was pissed off with the lot of them. They were taking him for a fool. He banged again, and then peered in through the thin curtains. All the lights were off. She was either out or asleep. He banged again. Nothing.

She needed a lesson. They all did. He took an empty fag packet from his pocket and drenched it in lighter fuel. Setting it alight, he then hurriedly shoved the burning cardboard through the letterbox. That'd teach the bitch.

Chapter 9

Jake was sitting at the kitchen table, working his way through a pile of exercise books. Beside him, in his highchair, was his eighteen-month-old son, Harry. The child was trying to feed himself, and getting the food everywhere but in his mouth.

Ruth looked across at them from the washing machine. "Give him a hand. Poor mite hasn't got the hang of it yet."

"These need doing tonight." Jake slapped the book he'd been marking down onto the table. "I can't concentrate in here. We need a study."

Same old, same old. Jake's attitude had gotten beyond a joke. Ruth looked at the man she lived with, the man who'd fathered her son. He was good-looking, intelligent. She'd fallen for him immediately. It seemed like a lifetime ago now. Ruth continued sorting through a pile of clean washing and heaved a sigh. Where had it all gone wrong? The romance had simply evaporated from their relationship, like steam from a kettle. There were days now when Ruth truly disliked Jake Ireson.

"What you need, sunshine, is a change of attitude long before we even consider a study. Anyway, where would we put it?"

Jake grunted. "There's nothing wrong with my attitude. I have to work, so I need the space. That's all."

"We don't have a spare bedroom. So it's either here or in the shed."

"Now you're being facetious."

"No, Jake. What I am is fed up. You do this night after night. I get a couple of words out of you at most. These days you mope around with a face I just want to punch!"

He got up. "I'll go work in the bedroom. Try to keep Harry quiet when you sort him for bed."

"You sort him! For God's sake, Jake, I've worked all day too. And I did the shopping, and I cooked your tea. I was hoping for an hour or two of down-time."

Harry started to cry. His face crumpled, and the tears rolled down his plump cheeks. "Look what you've done now," Jake snapped. "Happy with yourself?" He scooped up the books and hurried off. He mounted the stairs two at a time and slammed the bedroom door shut behind him.

Ruth flopped down into the chair beside Harry. She offered a spoonful of lukewarm food to the child. "Here you are, sweetie. Daddy's in one of his moods again, silly sod." Harry laughed and tried to snatch the spoon from her hand. "Independent streak, eh? We'll have to watch that." Ruth kissed his nose. Harry giggled and grabbed at his tea with his fingers.

This thing with Jake was getting no better. He refused to do anything with Harry. His head was always buried in a pile of books. Ruth couldn't go on like this. These arguments weren't fair on the child. She didn't want Harry growing up in a home where his parents were constantly at each other's throats. She'd have to have a serious talk with him, and the sooner the better.

* * *

It was gone eleven at night. As soon as he heard Ruth's ringtone, Jake began to make disapproving noises. For two pins, she'd blast him, but Harry had been cranky and she didn't want their raised voices waking him up now he'd finally gone down.

The call was from Calladine. He sounded fed up.

"There have been a couple of incidents on the Hobfield. Bernie Logan has been hospitalised. He was found outside Heron House, beaten and unconscious. And someone tried to torch Dolly Appleton's flat. As if she doesn't have enough on her plate."

"Someone's been busy," said Ruth.

"I'd lay odds it was Sean Hopwood. No one saw anything at Dolly's flat, but we might be in with a chance once Logan comes round."

"Was there much damage?"

"Thankfully not. A neighbour raised the alarm but the blaze had already burnt itself out on the mat just inside the door. There was a lot of smoke, that's all. Fortunately Dolly was unharmed."

"Shall I meet you at the hospital?"

"No, no, I've rung to keep you informed, that's all. I can manage on my own. I'm thinking Harry and all that stuff."

"*All that stuff* is sitting beside me now, sulking."

It was meant to be amusing, but Jake didn't see the joke. With a face like thunder, he grabbed a book and made for the stairs. "Jake is being a prima donna about his workload. He should try our job! No. I'll come. That man needs a lesson."

Ten minutes later, she was pulling out of the drive. Jake was looking after Harry whether he liked it or not. She had real work to do. She knew this was below the belt, Jake's job was important too. But he worked with school kids, hardly as tough as collaring murderous villains.

* * *

Calladine was waiting for her in the reception area of the emergency department. "He's come round. The nurse says we can see him once they've cleaned him up. He took a lot of vicious punches to the face and head. He was kicked several times, including one to the guts. They want to keep him in but he's refusing to stay. Worried about his flat, I think."

"Do we think it was the same person who set fire to Dolly Appleton's place?" Ruth asked.

"Forensics will help us work that out, hopefully. My money's on Hopwood. Both Logan and Dolly are clients of his."

She shook her head. "So is most of that estate."

"Ricky was having trouble getting his money earlier. Dolly couldn't pay, remember?"

Ruth made no comment. "Where was she when it happened?"

"She was asleep in bed. Her GP had given her a sedative. She was lucky, it could have been much worse. I've got uniform looking for Sean Hopwood. All we need is for Logan to tell us the truth and we've got him."

They walked along the quiet hospital corridors to a side room where Bernie Logan lay recovering.

"Who did you upset, Mr Logan?" Calladine peered at the man's face and saw the bruise rapidly spreading across one temple. He could have been killed. This level of violence was way over the top. "Someone meant business. You were lucky to get out alive."

"Got nowt to say. Didn't see the bastard. Crept up behind me." Bernie turned his face away.

Calladine heaved a sigh. "Didn't he say anything? Surely you must have some idea of who your attacker was?"

"No, not a clue. Like I said, swiped me from behind."

Calladine didn't believe him for a minute. "You weren't the only one targeted. Dolly Appleton was lucky not to have her flat burnt down. Lighted paper, or something like it, was pushed through her letterbox."

"Nowt do with me. It was dark. He were a big bugger. That's all I know."

"Did he rob you, Mr Logan?" Ruth asked.

"No, lass. Got nowt worth having."

Calladine shook his head. "You've got Hopwood chasing your tail. You haven't paid your debts. Dolly is in the same boat. Did he threaten you?"

Logan squinted against the bright light of the cubicle. "That bastard threatens everyone. Doesn't mean he does owt about it. Hopwood gets paid when we can afford it. He knows the score."

Calladine leaned forward. "You see, what bothers me, Mr Logan, is that this situation could escalate. I'm sure you are like me. You don't want to see anyone get killed."

"I know what you're doing, copper. But it won't wash. Someone gave me a beating. I didn't see him. I don't know if it was Hopwood or not. The lighting on that estate ain't up to much, as you know."

"Tell us what happened and we will put a stop to the intimidation."

Bernie snorted, and winced. "No you won't. You'll try, but you'll get nowhere. Blokes like Hopwood are police-proof."

"Very well, if that's how it is, we'll leave you in peace. Let's hope for your sake that Hopwood cools down. It doesn't look like you're up to defending yourself at the moment."

Calladine and Ruth left the room and went down the corridor towards the exit.

"Do we speak to Dolly?" asked Ruth.

Calladine shook his head. "No. We'll speak to her tomorrow."

"Why do they protect Hopwood, Tom? Why not just come clean and let us get the villain banged up?"

"Fear, I suppose. If we don't get it right, if he walks from court because of some technicality, they're in double trouble. Anyway, get rid of Sean and there is still Ricky to contend with. As yet he's an unknown, but he is a Hopwood, and he's had his big brother to teach him the trade. I don't doubt he'll be just as troublesome given time."

Ruth sighed. "Fancy a coffee or something?"

"Thought you'd want to dash off back to domestic bliss. I felt guilty enough as it was, dragging you out at this hour."

Ruth rolled her eyes. "Bliss! Huh. Far from it. Jake and I had another spat tonight. He's so into his job and those students of his that he won't give his family any time or consideration. And you didn't drag me out, I volunteered. Truth is, I'm losing it with him, Tom."

Calladine saw the sadness in Ruth's eyes. She was upset. She'd had high hopes for her relationship with Jake. She'd been unsure about committing herself to start with, but she'd gone ahead. It was looking like she might have been right in the first place. But now things were more complicated. They'd bought a house together and of course, they had Harry. Ruth couldn't simply walk away.

They sat at a table in the deserted hospital canteen. "I'm on the brink of taking Harry and leaving Jake to it. It might teach him a lesson. Though I doubt whether he'd even miss us. Jake would simply heave a sigh of relief and get on with his schoolwork. Plus, we've nowhere to go."

Calladine sat facing her. "He's not that hard-hearted. He'll be stressed. It's no picnic, you know, teaching them kids."

"It's not a lot of fun for us either most of the time. Look at the villains we have to deal with. Currently we've got the murder of a young girl, a cold case and now this little lot. Give me thirty teenagers any day. But he doesn't see that."

"You really are cut up, aren't you?" Ruth looked close to tears. Calladine averted his eyes. He'd no idea what to say or do. Last time, when they'd found Imogen, he'd got it all wrong. He looked across at her. "If things get really bad and you have to get away, you can always come to mine."

Her face brightened. "Are you being serious, Tom? Because if you are, I might just take you up on the offer. But you have to know up front that Harry is noisy, messy and can howl the place down at times. You might regret it."

Calladine laughed. "Won't bother me. I've got the big back bedroom and a small box-room. They're yours if it helps. Not that I'm encouraging you to leave Jake, mind. I really don't want to see that happen."

Ruth ignored this. "What about Shez? I know she stays over. Won't she mind? It'll take the gloss off those romantic nights in, a screaming kid and dirty nappies."

Calladine fumbled in his coat pocket and pulled out his mobile. "Here, look at this." He handed it to Ruth and watched her face as she read the message. She looked puzzled.

She handed the phone back. "What does it mean?"

"It means I've been dumped, and by text too." He tutted. "Got that a week ago but didn't want to say anything. Felt a bit foolish, to be honest. It was never going to last, was it? In the end, she got fed up with my job. A bit like you with Jake." He gave a small laugh.

"I'm sorry, Tom. You should have told me. I do understand."

"You'd have made fun of me like always. We've been here before, don't forget." He saw Ruth roll her eyes and knew just what she was thinking. He grinned. "Go on, say it."

Ruth chuckled. "I was trying to count up just how many times we have been here, Tom. You're a bloody loon, d'you know that!"

Chapter 10

Tuesday

It was early, not quite light. There were very few people about. The barren square between the tower blocks was empty. Hardly anyone around here worked, so there wasn't a lot to get up for. Dolly Appleton kept to the shadows. She didn't want to be seen.

The crisp morning air made Dolly shiver. She was tired. She'd had a long, traumatic night. She'd been fast asleep when a neighbour had come and told her about the fire. The man next door had hammered on her window until she'd finally stirred. Fortunately the fire had burned itself out on the doormat. But she'd still had to get up and sort her smoke-filled flat. Once she'd tidied things up, she'd dozed in a chair, terrified that whoever had done it might come back for a second go. The note had been waiting when she'd woken up. There was no signature. It seemed she was not the only one who was heartily sick of Hopwood's strong-arm tactics.

They were to meet in the cricket club. There was a small area at the back, behind the bar. No one would disturb them this early in the day. Dolly had read the note and made her mind up straight away. Whoever had sent this was right. Something had to be done about Sean Hopwood. He, or she, wrote that there would be five of them. Dolly was to come alone, and not to say a word to another living soul. That left her wondering what they had planned. She shivered again. Well, whatever it was, they were right. The man was an animal. If that fire hadn't burnt itself out, if she'd been in and asleep — which she was — what chance would she have had then?

The cricket field was overgrown, the grass wet and slippery. Dolly tramped towards the building. It looked empty and there were no lights on. She grew uneasy, unsure of what to do. Dolly had no idea what she was getting herself into. If Hopwood found out that people were meeting to discuss him, he'd lash out even more.

Then she saw a face at the window, watching her. It was an elderly man from the estate, called Frank. Smiling, he beckoned her in. That was a relief. Frank was someone ordinary, someone she knew. It helped to dissipate some of her fear and indecision.

"Come in and join us," another voice said.

Encouraged, she pushed open the door. Another wave of doubt overcame her when she realised the voice belonged to Bernie Logan. He was sitting at a table with three other people. Bernie had a reputation for getting into trouble. He was known for being handy with his fists. But her qualms disappeared when she saw his face. Dolly winced. The poor man had been badly beaten. His face was black and blue, his right eye was swollen and he had stitches at his temple.

He nodded at her. "Got this little lot last night. I've just discharged myself from hospital. I was targeted by Hopwood, like you. But you were lucky. The fire came to nowt. Next time we might not be so fortunate. What's the betting he kills one of us before much longer?"

A chorus of voices followed his words.

Dolly raised her voice above the noise. "Lucky? I hardly think so. I nearly lost everything. And my daughter not long dead! Don't forget that! To be honest, I don't know what I'm doing here. I don't see where talk will get us. Hopwood is an animal, but I haven't got the strength left in me to fight him."

Bernie looked at her. "That's why we need to stick together, Dolly. We can get the better of Hopwood by working together. Hopwood won't stop. He'll carry on with his bully-boy tactics until we crack. The bastard tried to burn your place down. You could easily have ended up dead like your girl, and he wouldn't have cared."

"It was Hopwood? You're sure?" But Dolly knew the answer already.

Logan nodded. "He did this to me. Before I passed out, the last thing I remember was him haring off up the stairs. He did me, then he came after you. The bastard is getting worse. Now he's got that brother of his on board. Hopwood needs fixing before he kills someone."

Dolly looked around. Bernie Logan, Frank, plus a man and a woman she knew only by sight. What was their story? Dolly wondered.

"We need rid of him," Bernie Logan stated. "The police won't or can't, but even if they arrested him, Hopwood would be back. He's got that brother of his to do his dirty work for him. He'll orchestrate things from his prison cell if he has to."

Dolly fastened her eyes on Logan's face. "What do you mean, 'rid of him?'"

"What I said. The estate would be a better place if Sean Hopwood was got rid of — for good." They looked at one another in silence. "He has to die, Dolly," Logan said simply.

"You can't be serious, none of you." She looked round at their solemn faces. No one was joking. "You really mean to get rid. To, to . . . *kill* him?" Part of her thought it made sense, but the idea was still horrific. "He's a thug and, yes, he hurts people, but you're talking murder. We'll never get away with it."

"Yes, we will." It was the man she knew only by sight. "We will, because we will do it right. We'll stick together and leave no trace."

Dolly shook her head. "You can't be sure of that. If we're caught, we'll all be locked up."

"If we don't do something to stop him, we'll end up dead." Bernie Logan sat back in his seat, as if there were nothing more to be said.

Dolly looked round at them. "So how do we go about it? Has anyone thought of that? Talking about killing is all very well, but someone has to actually carry it out."

"I'm John Barnett, a nurse," the man said simply.

Dolly looked more closely at him. Of course! That was where she knew him from. She'd seen him at the doctor's. "You live on the Hobfield?" He nodded. "And you've borrowed money from Hopwood?"

Logan spread his arms. "We all have. And none of us can keep up with the repayments. We all try, but the interest he charges is criminal. The longer we take, the more the debt grows, and the more violent Hopwood becomes."

"He's hurt Bernie here. He put Frank's wife in hospital," Barnett nodded at the older man, "and he's threatened me. Reckons by the time he's finished, I won't be fit to ever work again."

Frank looked at her. "He hurt my wife Annie real bad. She answered the door to him and he got into the flat." He had tears in his eyes. "He held her hand over a flame on the gas hob. Two of her fingers were badly burned. The doctors saved them but they're useless now. She still screams the place down with the pain. I'd kill the bastard myself if I had the strength."

Dolly was horrified. What Frank had just described was barbaric. "We should go to the police. They will help.

They will arrest him. We can all give evidence. Tell them what we know."

Frank shook his head. "It won't stick. We need witnesses to stand up and say they saw Hopwood do it. There aren't any. Some smart alec barrister would make mincemeat out of Annie's statement. She'd be no good in the witness box. Apart from which she's too scared to say anything. She reckons Hopwood will come back and do even worse. She's scared he'll hurt me next."

Logan looked at Dolly. "We asked you to join the group because you have suffered too. You don't know what happened to your girl. But she was seeing that thug's kid brother, Ricky."

Dolly closed her eyes. Is that what people thought? Did everyone on the estate think Ricky had killed Flora? "I hate Hopwood every bit as much as you. I owe him money, and I can't pay. But murder?"

Dolly knew the right thing to do was to get up and leave. They had to be mad to have come up with something like this. It would never work. But she was curious. The notion of ridding the estate of Hopwood was very appealing. "How can we hope to get away with it? The police will investigate. They'd find evidence. We all have a motive to want the man dead, some of us more than others. How can you be so sure that we'd be okay?" She looked at the nurse.

"Because we will devise a cast-iron plan."

Dolly shook her head. "That will take time. Meanwhile, anything could happen to any one of us."

Barnett spoke slowly. "I have thought of a way to kill him. But we need to work out the details."

Dolly's curiosity was aroused. "Go on."

"Put simply, Hopwood will be sedated, and then he will be given an overdose of insulin. He will die in his sleep."

Dolly shook her head. "You make it sound so easy. But how do we get the drugs — the insulin for example?"

"I will supply it. I'm a nurse. I have access to such things."

"You'll be found out." This whole thing was madness. "Drugs are monitored, logged. You can't just wander up to a drugs cabinet and help yourself."

"That's a risk I'd be willing to take. I can cover it up. I have done so before, when a colleague made a mistake. We're desperate, remember. Hopwood won't stop terrorising us. Once I've got the stuff, it's foolproof."

"You really mean to do this, don't you?" Dolly stared at him. He met her gaze steadily, and nodded. He meant it. They all did. They planned to kill Sean Hopwood and they wanted her in on it.

Dolly was appalled, but at the same time it made an odd sort of sense. Barnett had been right. Hopwood was a real threat to all of them.

"It'll take too long. Hopwood needs getting rid of quick."

Dolly could see that Bernie Logan was getting frustrated. "All this poncing about, getting hold of drugs and such." Logan looked at Barnett. "It's no bloody good. What's needed is for someone to get in close, knife the bugger — job done!"

There was uproar.

Barnett called out above the noise. "No one must act on their own. We need to work on our alibis, sort out who is going to vouch for who."

"I've heard enough." Logan got up and limped to the door. "You're a bunch of amateurs. I'll talk to you again when you've got a proper plan."

Dolly shook her head. "He's a hothead, but he has a point. Hopwood is after every one of us. We are not safe."

Barnett looked at her. "Are you suggesting we do what Bernie said?"

"No. The truth is, I don't know what to do. But we are plotting murder. Do you all realise what that means?" She looked at each one of them in turn. They looked back, frightened, desperate people who were willing to go to any lengths to be rid of Hopwood. "If the police get wind of this they will throw the book at us. It will be no use making excuses. We planned it. It is cold-blooded murder, pure and simple. We will all go down for a long time."

"He's a cold-blooded killer, Dolly." Barnett looked at her intently.

Dolly frowned. "As far as I'm aware, he hasn't actually killed anyone yet."

"Your daughter?" said Barnett. "You can't be sure it wasn't one of the Hopwoods that killed your Flora."

If Dolly could be certain of his guilt, she'd kill Sean Hopwood herself. With her bare hands if she had to.

Barnett looked round at them. "We will leave it there for now. Go away and think about what we have discussed. Hopwood must die, and soon."

"It sounds scary when you put it like that." Dolly shivered.

"We are all in this together. We have each other's backs. Are there any questions?" He looked at each of them in turn.

They all sat in silence, looking down at the table.

Then Dolly spoke up. "What if, when the time comes, we can't do it?" She looked at the nurse. "What if you bottle it?"

"That won't happen. We are all here because of what Hopwood has done to us or our loved ones. Just remember that, and how much you hate him. That man deserves all he's going to get."

Dolly was still unconvinced. This was wrong, morally wrong. They were conspiring to murder someone, take a life. Frank handed the nurse a piece of wire with two keys dangling from it. "One's for the main door and the other is for the locker. If you go ahead and get the insulin, you can put it in the locker. This place is empty all day until six in the evening, so you can come and go as you like."

Dolly looked at the others. These people were no different from her. They had all suffered Hopwood's brutality. She closed her eyes. Could she be part of this, even for Flora's sake? Dolly just wasn't sure.

Chapter 11

The following morning, Calladine arrived at the nick to find a message waiting for him. Short and to the point. Julian Batho wanted to see him urgently. Calladine picked up the phone. "We'll be at the Duggan for the Flora Appleton post-mortem," he said. "I'll pop along once it's finished."

"What I have to show you is in regard to the Jessica Wilkins case. I have found something that will both shock and surprise you," Batho said.

"Care to share it with me now?"

Calladine was impatient. He'd waited a very long time for a break on this case. But Julian wouldn't discuss it over the phone. It was delicate, apparently. Calladine would have to wait.

Ruth was reading through the Jessica Wilkins case notes. Julian's findings would mean that their meagre resources were stretched to the limit. They would be forced to give the case more input.

Nigel Hallam had arrived good and early. He offered no word as to what had taken him away yesterday, and Calladine didn't ask. He felt guilty for not giving the new

DC more of his time, but he found it hard to talk to him. Nigel looked the part, he made all the right noises, but something just wasn't right. Calladine still hadn't taken to him, and that wasn't like him. Nigel was continuing his research into the previous owners of the house on Beardsell Terrace. He sat with his eyes glued to his computer screen.

Calladine looked at Ruth. "We should get going." He called out to Nigel, "The minute you get anything on the house, text me."

They clattered down the stairs and out to the car. Ruth got into the driver's seat. "Alright. What's bothering you?"

"Julian's found something on the Jessica case. We're going to be snowed under very soon."

"No, it's more than that." She thought for a moment. "You don't like him, do you?"

So Ruth had noticed. "Just drive."

"We're all the same with him, you know. I think it must have something to do with Imogen. None of us can get it out of our heads that he's only here because she can't be, and we resent him for it. Childish, but there you are. It's human nature, I guess."

Calladine shook his head. "I feel awful about how I am with him. And I think he's starting to notice. In all the weeks he's been here, I don't think we've had a single conversation that wasn't work related. There's no small talk, no banter, just work stuff."

"Give it time. It'll settle."

"I don't think it will, Ruth."

"Well, it's too late now. He's in post, and he's not bad at the job either."

"Apart from his disappearing acts." Calladine frowned.

"Give the lad a break, Tom. If you want to know what Nigel's up to, it's simple — ask him!"

* * *

The two detectives looked down from the viewing platform above the post-mortem room — a grim spectacle. Covered from the neck down by a white sheet, Flora Appleton was laid out on a table. Her head looked grotesque, bloated. Eyes that had once been a clear blue bulged from their sockets.

Natasha Barrington must have heard Ruth gasp. "Lying for a week in a hot, confined space will do that to a person," she called up.

Ruth looked away. "I shouldn't have eaten breakfast. I think I'm going to throw up."

Calladine didn't feel much better but said, "If it's too much, I can do this alone."

Ruth cast him a glance. "You don't look great yourself. Let's just get it over with. I hate these things, but let's face it, we have been here before."

Indeed they had. Calladine had lost count of the number of times he'd stood watching while some unfortunate had been cut open and gutted. He sighed. Perhaps he was getting too old for all this.

Natasha Barrington pulled back the sheet. "I have had a closer look at the body. Dental records confirmed her identity. Given the state of the remains, the cause of death wasn't immediately obvious. As you can see, putrefaction is well advanced. When that happens the skin tends to slough away."

Calladine averted his eyes. The body had a distinct greenish-black tinge. It had once been a teenage girl, with her whole life in front of her. Whoever did this, whoever callously took her life and then dumped her, deserved all that was coming to them.

"However, on closer examination I discovered the knife wound that killed her just here." Natasha Barrington pointed with a gloved hand to the diaphragm, slightly below Flora's breasts. "The blade wasn't too long, but it was serrated."

"Like a steak knife?" Ruth asked.

Natasha nodded. "Yes, that would do it. There are several stab wounds as well. This was a frenzied attack and she put up a fight. The person responsible for the girl's death will show signs of it. At the very least, he or she will have a number of cuts and abrasions. Flora's knuckles are bruised."

The smell was getting to Calladine. At the first lengthways cut into the body, he felt decidedly queasy.

"The fatal stab wound entered the heart." Natasha held the organ cupped in her hands. "Death would have been quick."

"Given that she fought with her attacker, will you be able to get anything from under her fingernails?" Ruth asked.

Natasha tilted her head. "Decomposition allowing, we'll try. Forensics are examining her clothing, and of course the car. However, there was no handbag or mobile found."

Ruth nodded. "The killer may have taken it. Perhaps they sent that text to her mother."

"The clothing was in a state, I'm afraid. Blood had soaked into everything," said Natasha.

Calladine had had enough. He touched Ruth's arm. "I'm going to go and have that word with Julian. I'll meet you outside."

* * *

Julian was in his lab. He had the ashes spread out on a table and had removed several larger pieces of bone to study through his microscope.

He looked up at Calladine. "You're looking very grey."

Calladine shook his head. "Is it any wonder? I've just come from Flora Appleton's PM. She was stabbed and left in the boot of that car. All I have to do now is find the bastard that did it."

"We are looking at the car along with the girl's things, Tom. I'll have something for you very soon. In the meantime, here's something else to think about." He gestured to the table. "There was bone among those ashes you brought me, so we should get DNA. But I've found something else, something important." He pointed to a particular sample. "What you're looking at is part of the skull, see the slight curve and the thinness of the bone?"

Calladine peered down at it. The bone was a few centimetres in size. A regular semi-circular piece on one edge was missing.

Julian pointed at it. "I'm trying to find more, but it's a bit like doing a jigsaw puzzle. There are dozens of bits of bone but I doubt I'll find a match for that particular one."

Calladine grimaced. "A grisly jigsaw. What is so significant about it?"

"The slice out of the piece you're looking at was made by a bullet. It's an entry wound."

Calladine shook his head. This didn't make any sense. "What? Who would shoot a toddler? Are you absolutely sure, Julian?"

"I can't see what else would have left such a regular hole. You've seen enough bullet holes in your time. What do you think?"

"What I'm thinking is, who would want to put a gun to a child's head? It beggars belief." The disappearance of Jessica Wilkins had haunted him for years. But this! Julian's discovery added yet another horrific dimension to the case. "The child was supposed to have disappeared from Leesdon Park. Now it looks as if whoever took her shot her through the head. It's certainly not what I expected."

"It entered the skull about here." Ignoring these remarks, Julian pointed to his own forehead. "And exited at the back. The exit wound would have shattered the skull, but the entry wound is quite neat. I've also found parts of the femur and one or two bits of vertebrae. We're lucky that particular piece of skull was still intact."

This news was huge. Calladine couldn't risk it getting out. "We'll keep this to ourselves for the time being. Can you imagine what the press would make of it?" Again, there was no comment from Julian.

Instead, he said, "We are still searching the house on Beardsell Terrace."

"Anything?"

"Early days. CSI officers have brought a few things back. Mostly rubble from around where the jar was found, plus these." Julian passed him several evidence bags containing pieces of pink silk fabric. "It looks as if these were used as packing around the container. Expensive fabric. Someone took a great deal of care to ensure it stayed safe. The officers also found this." He handed Calladine a bag containing a gold crucifix. "It's eighteen carat, also expensive. But there is no inscription unfortunately."

"All carefully placed and left with this." Calladine held up the bag. "It suggests someone who cared for the child. And why that house? I wonder what its significance is."

Julian shrugged. "Your department, I think. I'm working on the DNA, but it will be a while. The blanket yielded three infant hairs, blonde."

Calladine nodded. Little Jessica had been blonde. "Thanks, Julian. I'll get back now. Keep this quiet. If those are Jessica's ashes, it means that someone shot her. I just can't get my head around that one. Who would do such a thing for a start? Over the last two decades there have been three children murdered in Oldston. All different killers, but on each occasion the child was smothered. I've never heard of a shooting."

Julian didn't react at all. "If I discover anything further, I'll let you know."

It was a strange one and no mistake. Julian was a worry too. He'd kept it all so business-like. Not that he'd ever been overly chatty, but they could usually get something out of him.

He found the PM room locked. Ruth was coming out of the toilets. She looked as white as a sheet.

She coughed. "Afraid I've lost my breakfast. That one has to go to the top of the list. Natasha has finished. She says the report will be up later today, bar the results of the forensic tests."

"I've decided to speak to a couple of people again with regard to the Jessica Wilkins case. I'll give you a lift back to the station first though. You look a bit ropey."

"I'll be fine. It was a combination of a late night, the smell in there, and the fact that she was so young. Did Julian tell you anything interesting?"

Calladine decided that now wasn't the time. Ruth had had enough for one morning. "It might be something. I'll tell you later. You sure you're alright?"

"I'll be fine. A strong cuppa will sort me out."

Chapter 12

Calladine decided to call and see Monika once he'd dropped Ruth off at the station. He wanted to ask her to run through her version of that afternoon's events one more time. Monika and he had history. They had been close once, and he'd even considered marrying her. But each time it looked as if they might make a go of it, another woman came along and turned his head. Ruth despaired of him.

Monika Smith was the manager of a care home on the outskirts of Leesdon. Calladine's mother had spent the last few years of her life there, and back then he had been a regular visitor. Today, the place felt alien. He strode across the car park and rang the front door bell, feeling nervous. The last time he'd seen Monika it hadn't gone well. The woman who answered the door smiled at him somewhat frostily.

Calladine returned her smile. "Is Monika in?"

"She is, but I'm not sure if she'll want to see you."

So Monika hadn't held back on telling her colleagues all the gory details of their on-off relationship. His smile faded. "Tell her it's police business."

"Wait in there." She pointed to a small waiting room.

Calladine went in. He stared out of the window with his hands in his overcoat pockets, wishing he hadn't come.

"What do you want?"

Monika stood in the doorway, staring at him, her arms folded. Calladine felt like a naughty child. "Hello, Monika. I'm sorry to interrupt if you're busy, but I wondered if you'd help me with something."

"With what, exactly? I am rather busy. Running this place for one."

She looked good. She'd lost weight and had her hair done in a new style. It was longer, reaching her chin, and it suited her. She obviously wasn't pleased to see him. Her voice was sharp, her body language, well, unwelcoming. He should have left well alone.

"Well, come on. I haven't got all day," she said.

"The Jessica Wilkins case. You gave a statement."

Her face fell. "That was years ago, Tom." She came into the room and closed the door behind her. "Why rake all that up? It'll just cause more pain. That poor woman. I can still see her now, running round frantically, screaming her head off."

Calladine looked at her. Would she be able to help? "So you remember that day?" She nodded. "How well, exactly? How much of the detail can you recall? Did you actually see the child, for example?"

"No, I didn't. Read the statement. The child was sleeping in her pushchair."

"How do you know that?"

Monika looked puzzled. "What do you mean, Tom? It's obvious, isn't it? Josie Wilkins comes onto the park. She sits down with the pushchair beside her. I don't know how long she stayed. I was busy. We'd taken some of the residents there for some fresh air and Mr Johnson went walkabout. I spent a good thirty minutes or so looking for him. By the time I got back, it was all cracking off."

"Where did you find him?"

Monika tutted. "In the Wheatsheaf, with a double whiskey in his fist. Made him as sick as a dog. Didn't agree with his medication. Silly old fool!"

"And there's nothing else?"

"No. Much later we heard on the local news that the child had been taken. I wish I could recall something useful, Tom, I really do. At the time I racked my brain, went over it several times. But neither I nor the nurse who was with me saw anything untoward."

"The nurse, does she still work here?"

"No, Tom, she died three years ago. But you should have her statement."

"Did she go looking for Mr Johnson too?"

"No, she stayed put," Monika replied.

"Do you recall if she said anything about actually seeing the child herself?"

"She couldn't remember. She had her hands full with me going off like that. Why are you so bothered, Tom?"

"The case has been reopened. New evidence has come to light. I was filling Ruth in, and it was something she suggested. I did consider it at the time, but Josie Wilkins was so distraught I thought she couldn't possibly have been making it up."

Monika frowned. "What are you getting at?"

"Ruth suggested that the child was never in the pushchair in the first place."

Monika looked at him. "Ruth thinks the park thing was staged? Part of some elaborate plan to cover up something else, perhaps what had really happened?"

"Yes, I think that's what she's getting at."

"Clever girl, our Ruth."

"The trouble is, Monika, I can't find anyone who actually saw the child in the flesh. There is nothing in the statements. So naturally it got me thinking. It's something that should have been pursued at the time, but it wasn't. And I still can't work out Josie's part in it. Everything about her reactions that day was spot on. All that emotion was real. She genuinely believed her daughter had been taken."

"I don't doubt it. But you did consider her state of mind?"

"What d'you mean?"

"Josie Wilkins had problems long before her daughter went missing. Her grandfather was a resident here for a while. He wouldn't have anything to do with her. Reckoned that most of the time, Josie was off her head on drugs. He told me that Jessica was born with heroin dependency."

That was twice now that someone had referred to Josie's drug problem. Calladine knew nothing about it. "She was a single parent. We checked with social services, and there was nothing untoward. Surely something like that would have been flagged up?"

Monika shrugged. "I'm simply telling you what the old fella told me."

"If Jessica had problems at birth, they would have needed sorting."

"You'll have to ask at the hospital. What's the new evidence?"

"Jessica's ashes have been found."

Monika stared at him with wide eyes. "No! After all this time? I don't know what to say. Ashes. That's dreadful. What on earth happened to her? Are your forensic people able to tell how she died?"

"Yes, and that makes it doubly dreadful." He looked at her. "I can't say anything more. We have to keep it quiet for the time being."

Monika nodded, and changed the subject tactfully. "I understand. You're looking well, Tom. Keeping up the healthy living?"

"After a fashion. It's walking the dog that does it. Marilyn, Ray's wife, left me her dog, Sam, when she was banged up. I didn't get a chance to refuse. It was either take the dog on or get him put down. He's okay, though, no trouble at all."

She smiled. "The look suits you. How are Ruth and the team? Are you all coping after what happened to Imogen?"

"Just about. It's not easy. We miss her, simple as that."

"Well, I must get on. Give Ruth my best. Tell her I'll ring her, we're due a catch-up."

"Thanks, Monika. We might have to talk again."

"You know where I am."

After the initial cold reception, Monika had seemed happy enough to talk. She'd even been quite friendly. Smiled once or twice too. Calladine was confused all over again. He'd never been able to work out how he really felt about Monika.

He drove off in the direction of Leesdon centre. He'd pay a visit to Beardsell Terrace. He ought to check out where the ashes had been found, see how forensics were getting on. He knew exactly where it was, only three streets away from his place.

* * *

A team of four from the Duggan, headed up by Roxy Atkins, were hard at work. The sitting room was in a state. The team certainly hadn't held back. Where the fireplace had been was now a huge hole in the wall, made even bigger by their searching.

Calladine surveyed the mess. "Found anything else?"

Roxy shook her head. "Nothing. The place is clean. Interestingly, I'd say the space for the ginger jar was made deliberately. See here." She pointed to a hole in the back wall of the fireplace. "You can literally lift out the bricks, the mortar between them is perished. But just here someone made an oblong-shaped hole, then bricked up the front. You are looking into who lived here at the time?"

Calladine nodded. "DC Hallam is researching that as we speak."

"That's your best bet then. I doubt we'll get much more here."

"No chance of a bullet then?"

Roxy Atkins looked at him, and frowned. "Not unless the kid was killed here. It wasn't found in the ashes, so I expect it is still lodged wherever."

Calladine's mobile rang. It was Ruth.

"We have a nasty incident, Tom, on the Hobfield, at Heron House. It's Sean Hopwood. He's been stabbed and pushed from the first-floor deck." There was a pause. "He's dead, Tom," Ruth said.

"Stabbed, you said? Like Flora Appleton."

Chapter 13

Dolly Appleton had walked slowly back to her flat in a daze, going over everything in her mind. They were right, the lot of them. Sean Hopwood deserved everything that was coming to him. He was a thug who gave no quarter. Dolly shuddered when she thought of what he'd done to Frank's wife.

She arrived home, locked the door behind her and pulled the curtains tight shut. With Flora gone, Dolly was alone. If that brute Hopwood came knocking again, it would look as if she was out. The sooner they got this over and done with, the better. There was no going back. It was already too late anyway. She'd sat down with the others and planned to commit murder. She was in this right up to her neck.

Minutes later, and with a mug of tea in her hand, her thoughts turned to the where and the when. There remained the question of whether she was capable of doing it. Could she take another human being's life, even if that person was Hopwood? The short answer was, no. In that case she'd have to withdraw. She'd have to tell the others she was sorry, but it had been a terrible mistake.

Dolly sat down at the table and burst into tears. She was no killer, none of them were. But as the minutes ticked by and she continued to think about it, the less she could see an alternative.

The nurse had said within a couple of days. Even as she sat here, the others were thinking about the method, the location and how to get Hopwood alone. They would need alibis, too. Dolly was shaking. If she took part in this, the police would come for her. If she was locked up and questioned she'd cave in, tell them everything. Then they'd all get locked up.

What Dolly needed was the guts to see it through. She closed her eyes and thought of Flora. Her daughter had been dumped in the boot of that car like a piece of rubbish. Rumours were going around the estate like a whirlwind. Word had it that Ricky Hopwood was involved somewhere. He and Flora had argued. Everyone in the Pheasant had heard them. That young man had caused untold heartache and damage, but he was walking around scot-free. He hadn't even been interviewed by the police! Whatever those thugs Kyle Logan and his friends had told them, it would have been nothing like the truth. Neither of the Hopwood brothers had had any sympathy for poor Flora. They deserved everything that was coming.

When Dolly reached her block, she realised something was up. About a dozen people had gathered in the square and a police car was in attendance. Ordinarily she would have gone over, found out what had happened. But she was shattered. It had been a long night, sorting her flat after the fire, finding out about Flora, and now this. She went into the sitting room and fell into a doze on the sofa.

Dolly hadn't been asleep for long when she was woken by the sound of voices and people shouting outside. Something must have happened earlier, hence the police car. She should go out, see what was going on, but she was too scared. What if it was Hopwood? The minutes ticked by. Dolly was jittery, and jumped at every sound.

She made a cup of tea and tried to calm down. Suddenly she heard an ambulance siren. It was getting louder, coming closer. Whatever had happened must be serious. She stepped out of her front door and looked over the rail. She saw a small white tent on the ground below with a couple of policemen standing guard.

One of the neighbours joined her. "A fight, her at the end said. She heard the bugger scream. It's Sean Hopwood. They think someone stuck a knife in him, then pushed him over the rail."

"Is he dead?" Dolly asked in a shaky voice.

"With any luck, but even if he's not, he'll be in a bad way."

"Have the police got anyone?" Dolly was really nervous now. Could it be one of the group? If it was, why hadn't they waited and discussed it with the others?

The neighbour shrugged. "No one saw. Don't think they'd say even if they had." A big grin spread across her face. "Whoever it was, they done the lot of us a favour."

* * *

A tent had been hastily erected to cover the body. People were craning their necks to see over the tape cordoning off an area a few metres from the entrance to Heron House. Apart from the comings and goings of the police, there wasn't much to see.

Calladine met Ruth at the scene.

She raised a finger. "Sean Hopwood. A knife in the back, then pushed from up there, first floor. Uniform are having a look. You can see where the railing has come away from the brickwork."

Calladine looked up, then followed an imaginary line downwards to the ground. The concrete around them was littered with pieces of broken metal and brick. He picked up a piece. The old railing was crumbling with rust.

"He landed heavily. Any number of people said they heard him smash onto the ground. There was nothing anyone could have done. Someone called an ambulance but the paramedics confirmed he'd already gone."

Calladine looked around. "Has anybody said anything? Anyone own up to seeing what happened?"

"Not yet. But according to the paramedic who looked at the wound, it seems Hopwood was jumped from behind, knifed and pushed over."

"So some idiot finally caught up with the crook. Can't say I'm surprised. The man was universally hated on this estate." Calladine shook his head.

"That doesn't make it right, though," Ruth reminded him. "It's still murder, and we have to find the killer."

Calladine pulled a face. A thankless task. He was surprised that no one had taken a pop at Hopwood before now. "It won't help us, the victim being Hopwood. The attacker could be anyone here, they all had a motive." A grim-faced Calladine walked towards the tent and went inside to talk to the CSIs.

One of them broke away from the group and took off his mask. "According to the bloke who rang it in, it happened less than an hour ago. We'll do a sweep of the area and the deck above. His clothing might yield something, fibres and the like. Knifed in the back. That means getting up close and personal."

"Okay, let me have the preliminary report as soon as." Calladine stepped out of the tent and beckoned to Ruth. "Better take a look up there. Someone might have seen or heard something. With a bit of luck they might even want to speak to us, although I won't hold my breath. Whoever did it will have hero status before long."

Ruth shook her head. "As if we didn't have enough on our plates. There's Bernie Logan for a start. He didn't say, but it was probably Hopwood who battered him yesterday. That gives him a motive."

"Also Dolly Appleton. Hopwood tried to burn her out. I'll be speaking to her, and the rest." Calladine sighed.

"Did you get anything useful on the back of what Julian told you?"

Calladine led her away from the others. "I spoke to Monika again, but she couldn't tell me anything different from what's in her statement."

Ruth looked at him. "So what *did* Julian tell you?"

"Something I certainly wasn't expecting." He frowned. Ruth wasn't going to like this. "Little Jessica was shot. She took a bullet to the head."

As he expected, Ruth was shocked. She gasped and grabbed his arm. "Sorry. For a second there I felt quite weird. First that bloody autopsy, and now this. It beggars belief, it's so horrible. Is he sure?"

"You know Julian. He doesn't joke about death. But not a word to anyone else. This information is sensitive and the media would love it. We don't want it getting out. We particularly don't want Josie and her sister finding out yet."

"She'll find out eventually, Tom. But who would do that to such a small child?"

Calladine shook his head. "I can't get my head around it."

There were tears in Ruth's eyes. "Sorry. My emotions seem to be all over the place."

"It's okay. Didn't do me a lot of good either." Calladine lifted his arm, but then let it drop. "Sorry. Thought you might like a hug. You being a mum of a small child and all that."

Ruth frowned. "Let's not bring all that up again, please. You don't have to hug me every time you bring bad news. I am quite tough, you know."

"But not lately?"

"It's been a hard few months."

There was an uncomfortable silence. After a while, Calladine said, "We're alright, the two of us, aren't we?"

"What do you mean?"

"Well, you know. That thing that happened when we found Imogen. You don't say much, but I sense you are wary around me now."

She looked at him. "How do you expect me to answer that one, Tom?"

He shrugged, and cleared his throat. "We're close. It's like I said at the time, I've known you longer than any other woman in my life currently. I didn't know my daughter, Zoe, existed until a couple of years ago. And as for my birth mother, Eve, well, you know how little I see of her."

"So what are you saying? That when things get tricky you have the right to fling your arms around me? Kiss me even?"

"See, I knew it. For reasons I still don't understand, what I did then upsets you."

Ruth looked into his eyes. "No, you're wrong. It confuses things, that's all. You're my boss. You're my friend too, and that's how I'd like it to stay if it's all the same with you. I certainly don't want our relationship to change — in any way. Boundaries, that's all we need." She nodded, as if to herself. "How about I'll try not to get emotionally needy, and you don't grab hold of me at every opportunity? That'll do for starters."

Why did that sound like a threat? Ruth was warning him off. Calladine changed the subject. "Someone will have to tell his brother, Ricky. Feel up to it? Free me up to speak to this lot." He nodded at the flats above.

"I'll take Nigel with me. See what he's made of."

"You can ask Ricky about his relationship with Flora too. Find out when he last saw her." He nodded towards the place where the old car had been parked. "But first I'm going to have a word with the CSI people down there. See if they've found anything useful."

"Don't forget it has been raining since the killing," Ruth warned him.

Chapter 14

Calladine's revelation about Jessica Wilkins had upset Ruth. During the last twenty-four hours she had considered a number of scenarios, but the thought that someone had shot the child through the head had never entered her mind.

Nigel Hallam broke the silence. "Hopwood won't be missed."

Ruth shook herself. She must keep her mind on the case in hand. "That's not the point. He's been murdered. Missed or not, we still have to do our job."

They were in Ruth's car, heading towards the edge of town and the Hopwood home.

"I remember Ricky from school," said Nigel. "He was an odd one."

"With a brother like Sean raising him, what do you expect? Both parents were dead by the time Ricky was three years old. Odd or not, he's as much a victim of Sean's brutality as anyone."

Nigel shook his head. "He won't take it well. He might think he's a big man, but he's still a kid really."

"He's going to have to step up now. God knows what kind of mess Sean has left behind him. And Ricky will have to run the business on his own. That's asking a lot from someone who's nowhere near as tough as his brother."

The Hopwood home was on the outskirts of the area known as Leesworth. It consisted of several villages, and the town of Leesdon. The Hopwoods lived in the tiny village of Hopeshaw. Stone terraced houses ran the length of the main road, with one or two larger houses dotted about the surrounding hillsides. The Hopwoods lived in one of these.

It was a huge stone pile hugging the side of a hill. Ruth pulled up in the driveway outside the front door and looked up at it. "This must have cost a fortune."

"No doubt it was bought with their ill-gotten gains," Nigel added. "The exorbitant interest charged on the few hundred poor folk borrow."

Ruth rang the doorbell. "Not that we can do anything about it, and that's the problem."

Ricky answered the door wearing a dressing gown and drying his hair with a towel. He recognised Nigel Hallam and pulled a face. "What d'you want? I'm busy."

Ruth spoke gently. "Ricky, can we come in? We need to talk to you. It's best done inside, and it's something that won't wait."

"No. Spit it out, then do one. Sean needs me on the job, so I don't have time for tea and biscuits with you lot."

The softly, softly approach was getting them nowhere. Alright, thought Ruth, we tried. "Sean has been killed, Ricky. He was attacked and stabbed earlier this morning. So whether you like it or not, we do need to speak to you."

Ricky froze. He slowly brought the towel from his head and let it drop. His eyes went from one detective to the other. Ruth saw the disbelief on his face. He was struggling with the news.

Finally, he shook his head. "You're having me on. Not our Sean. Where is this s'posed to have happened?"

"I'm afraid this is no joke, Ricky," Ruth replied. "He was found on the Hobfield."

"What happened? Who would dare? I've been telling him for ages to reel it in." He squinted at them, and his expression shifted from shock to suspicion.

Ruth shook her head. "We can't do this on the doorstep. We need to come in. We have to ask you a few questions, Ricky."

Woodenly, he moved aside.

The hallway was wide and long, the ceiling low with a thick oak beam running the length of it. Ricky led them into a sitting room. That too had a low, wood-beamed ceiling, and two tall leaded windows. Apart from a few pieces of antique stuff, the furniture was modern and colourful.

"What happened? Which of them scroats did for him?"

Ruth looked at him. "Sean was found this morning on the ground outside Heron House. He was stabbed and then fell or was pushed from the first floor. Whoever did that meant business. It was no half-hearted attempt."

"Stabbed? Fell? It doesn't make sense. No one would have the balls . . . Are you sure?"

"Yes. We wouldn't be here otherwise." Ruth lowered her voice. "This was murder, Ricky, and we need to catch whoever did it."

He looked at them, his eyes wide. "I warned the stupid bastard! The way he treated people. Sooner or later it was bound to get him into trouble."

Ruth moved a step towards him. "We are going to need your help, Ricky. We need to know everything about Sean's life. Who he'd upset, if there had been any threats. You know the stuff."

Ricky slammed his fist against the wall, and howled in pain. "No one liked Sean. Everyone on that damned estate wanted his blood. I knew he'd go too far one day."

Ruth nodded. "We do know about Sean's reputation. We know that he intimidated clients when they couldn't repay the loans they'd taken on. Had anyone threatened him recently? Did Sean go out this morning to see anyone in particular?"

"No, just the usual round. He was chasing up the non-payers. That happens on a weekly basis. I do the normal round, and Sean goes out to see the punters who avoided me. They need a sharp word, putting straight. Sean is better at that. We're a business, not a charity."

"Had Sean upset anyone who might retaliate?" Nigel asked.

Ricky didn't answer straight away. He was pacing up and down. "Sean just had to walk into a room to upset folk. People didn't like him. But I didn't think anyone would have the balls to do something about it."

Ruth took out her notebook. "This was murder, so someone did. In order to find out who that was, we need you to tell us one or two things. We need a list of your clients, particularly those who live in Heron House. We need to know who was behind on the repayments, who owed the firm the most."

"I was collecting at Heron House yesterday. There were lots of people who didn't pay, who wouldn't even answer the door. Sean went back last night to have a word with one or two of them, but he got nowhere."

Nigel moved closer to the pacing Ricky. "Did he have a 'word' with Bernie Logan? He was taken to A & E badly beaten."

"I don't know," was the sullen reply. "But Bernie was on the list. Sean was sick of him."

"What about Dolly Appleton? Someone tried to set fire to her flat last night," said Nigel.

Ricky flushed. He began to shout. "Now that he can't stick up for himself, you're trying to pin everything on Sean! That's the game, isn't it? You lot must think I'm daft."

Ruth sighed. "Okay, Ricky. Calm down. Where were you this morning?"

"Here. I've just got out of bed. You can't seriously think I'd harm my own brother?" He walked over to a computer sitting on a desk against the wall.

Ruth shrugged. "We have to ask. That's quite a bruise you've got on your cheek."

"Bumped into a door, didn't I?"

Ruth suspected it was more likely the lad had fallen foul of Sean's temper. She didn't push it.

Ricky handed Ruth a data stick. "Here. This do you? A list of everyone who currently has a loan with us. It's all there: names, addresses, amounts outstanding, the lot."

Ruth took the stick. "Thank you. It will be very helpful. Now, on a different subject, we've been told that you were seeing Flora Appleton."

Ricky shrugged. "Nothing serious. We had a drink from time to time, that's all."

Ruth raised her eyebrows. "You bought tickets to a music festival for the pair of you."

"So? Doesn't mean owt. She kept mithering. I got the tickets to shut her up. I never intended going."

Ruth smiled. "Okay. We'll talk about Flora another time."

Ricky looked at her, almost pleading. "What have you done with him? Where do I go if I want to see him?"

"He is at a place called the Duggan Centre," Ruth explained. "There will have to be a post-mortem and forensic tests done. If you want to see him, I can arrange for a uniformed officer to take you. Perhaps you'd like to tell people first, family for instance. Get someone to go with you."

He looked at Ruth for a few seconds, then shook his head. "There is no one."

* * *

Calladine stood on the first-floor deck with one of the scenes-of-crime officers.

The CSI gave the rail a shake. "It's made of metal, but it isn't in the best condition, is it? The whole lot is badly rusted. It wouldn't have taken much for it to give way like it did. These are old blocks. They've needed urgent repair for years. But what's the betting the council will bleat on about having no money?"

"So someone could have come up behind Hopwood, stabbed him, then a bit of a shove and down he went?"

The CSI nodded. "Sounds plausible. Hopefully the pathologist will get some answers. I must say, there is a lot of debris down there on the ground."

This was all speculation. Calladine needed the forensics results before he started concocting theories. He looked along the deck. The place was empty. The council had promised to fix it quickly, but in the meantime it was a death trap. He'd ring them, see if they'd at least cordon it off.

Uniform had already started on the door-to-door enquiries. Calladine didn't believe that Hopwood could have been knifed without anyone seeing. He checked his watch. Time to have a wander round. First, he'd take the lift up to the twelfth floor, check up on Josie Wilkins. The sight of uniformed officers would have got her spooked. Truth was, if a policeman came knocking most round here wouldn't even answer the door.

But Josie Wilkins wasn't hiding away. She was standing on the deck outside her flat, looking down at what was happening on the ground below.

She caught sight of Calladine. "I heard the noise. Arguing and screaming. Dreadful it was. I'd no idea what had happened. I heard the thud when he hit the concrete."

She shuddered. "I didn't look over. I guessed someone must have gone over the side."

He looked at her. "Are you okay? You look very pale."

"I've just heard some poor bastard get a kicking. Of course I'm not okay." Josie wrapped her arms around herself.

"It was worse than that, I'm afraid," Calladine said. "We'll go inside and I'll make us a cup of tea."

She inhaled deeply and led the way into her flat. "It's been an awful week so far. First Jess, and now this."

"Did you see any of what happened? Hear anything? Do you have any idea who the man was arguing with?"

She shook her head. "No. You can't see the lower decks from up here. But I heard the shouting."

Josie was deathly pale and still shaking from the shock. She didn't appear to know that it was Hopwood who'd been killed. He went into the small kitchen and switched the kettle on. "Tea bags do you?"

"All I use, love," she shouted back.

He popped his head around the door. "Are you up to talking, Josie? Can you tell me exactly what you heard?"

Josie buried her face in a cushion and began to weep. "I'm sick of it round 'ere. If I had the money, I'd disappear. Go somewhere nice, near the sea, and never come back!"

Calladine reappeared with two cups of tea. "Drink that. Might have a bit more sugar than you're used to, but it'll do you good."

She wiped her eyes and sniffed. "I heard blokes arguing. I didn't take much notice at first. Folk are always at it round 'ere. One of them told the other bloke to get lost. 'Yer'll get nowt more,' he said."

"What happened then?"

"More shouting, then a scream." Josie's voice trembled. "I was scared. They were several floors down but they were really screaming at each other. I didn't want them to see me so I came inside, and listened from the window. Then I heard one of them shriek and I came out again. Wish I hadn't, but I did. I'll never forget the noise he made." She paused to blow her nose. "Who was it?"

Josie would find out soon enough. It was all over the estate. "Sean Hopwood," he said simply. "He's dead."

"He was a bad bugger, but even he didn't deserve that. The way he was, I suppose someone was always going to try, sooner or later."

"Was anyone else with you, Josie?"

She shook her head.

"Did you see anyone on the lower decks looking over? Even the back of their heads?"

"No, there was no one. Whoever he was fighting with must have gone back into their flat, or legged it down the stairs."

Josie looked done in. "Do you want me to get Tracy?" asked Calladine. "I could ring her work, get her to come and sit with you."

She seemed to shrink. "She doesn't like it when I disturb her at work."

"She won't mind. You've had a bad week. You shouldn't be on your own. Do you have a number for her?"

Josie hesitated. She picked up her mobile off the table and held it to her chest.

"It'll be okay, she won't mind," Calladine assured her.

She found the number, and handed him the phone. "You speak to them. It's ringing."

"*Social Services.*"

Calladine asked to speak to Tracy Wilkins. Once he was put through, he told Josie's sister what had happened. Tracy sounded peeved, but finally agreed to come home.

Calladine left Josie and Heron House and walked towards the Pheasant pub. He passed two forensic officers on their knees, going over the hard concrete ground inch by inch.

One of them pointed down. "The concrete is worn away along here. The soil and weeds are coming through all over. Just here, though, there is a fresh bare patch, like a foot has scraped it away."

"You think this is where it happened?"

The officer pointed at his colleague. "He's just bagged up some hair and an earring he found, so yes. If the hair proves to be that of the murdered girl, I'd say we've found the spot. Busy round here today, isn't it?" The CSI nodded at Heron House.

"Bad time all round." Calladine looked about him. He and the CSIs were in the shadow cast by the tower blocks, just out of sight of the pub. With the poor lighting, and on a wet night, they'd be lucky to find anyone who saw what happened.

Chapter 15

The team arrived back at the station in the early afternoon. Calladine tidied up the incident board and wrote *Sean Hopwood* across the top. He was about to start the meeting when the incident room door opened. Rocco walked in. Calladine, Ruth and Joyce all shouted at once.

Ruth was smiling broadly. "Just in the nick of time, I reckon. We've got our hands full."

Rocco looked sideways at Calladine. "I legged it from the course. Hope you don't mind, sir. It wasn't up to much. The place was in the middle of nowhere and there was nothing going on at the hotel either."

Calladine smiled at him. "Plenty going on here. A young girl killed and dumped on the Hobfield, a cold case come to life again. And someone has just done for Sean Hopwood, local villain of this parish."

"Sorry." Rocco looked sheepish. "I feel bad about leaving you all like that, but I really needed a change of scene. I spoke to Long and he let me register for the course. I felt I had to put some space between me and you lot, from everyone who knew Imogen in fact. But now that I've had time to think, I know that running away wasn't the answer. I know things will never be the same. I just need to get down to work, get back into the usual routine."

Ruth nodded at him. "We know how you feel, Rocco. It's the same for all of us. I'm going about in a sort of daze. I still can't believe it happened."

Calladine smiled again. "If it's the *usual* you need, we're up to our eyes in it." He grew serious. "We're the medicine you need, Rocco. We have to work through this together, as a team. Help each other."

Calladine was very pleased to see Rocco back at the nick. The place didn't feel right without him. Losing Imogen was bad enough, but the idea that Rocco might want out too didn't bear thinking about. He completely understood how the young man felt. Rocco and Imogen had been friends, they'd joined CID at the same time.

He turned to the board, marker in hand. "Right then, let's get started. Sean Hopwood was found dead at the foot of Heron House on the Hobfield this morning." This was for Rocco's benefit.

"Hopwood the loan shark?" Rocco asked. "Used his fists to settle every beef, mostly about the money folk owed him?"

Calladine nodded. "That's him. Hopwood upset everyone he came across. No one on the Hobfield has a good word to say about him. Apart from it being murder, we are interested because Hopwood was stabbed, same as Flora Appleton. We have nothing yet to suggest it, but the two cases could be linked."

Ruth held up the data stick. "We spoke to his brother, Ricky, and gave him the bad news. He was surprisingly forthcoming. This has everything we need. He might have been a tough bruiser, but Hopwood did keep good records." She handed the data stick to Nigel, to produce a printed list for later. "Ricky told us that Sean went out this morning to chase up non-payers from the day before. He wasn't in the best of moods either."

Calladine picked up the thread. "We know that the two clients who were bugging Sean the most were Bernie Logan and Dolly Appleton. What we don't know is whether he caught up with them or not. Logan was attacked last night. He was beaten so badly he had to be taken to A & E. But he won't say who attacked him. Then someone tried to set fire to Dolly's flat. She is Flora's mother, another link to the Hopwoods." Calladine pointed to the incident board. "She maintains that she can't tell us who tried to torch the place. She says she doesn't know, but I'm not so sure. Those two have to go to the top of the list."

"We should speak to them again," said Ruth. "Get their alibis for this morning."

Calladine nodded. "I think we should do a sweep of Heron House, speak to everyone. There will be very few who kept to the fine print of the agreement they had with Hopwood."

"I agree, sir." Rocco looked eager to start immediately.

Ruth was less enthusiastic. "That's a lot of people to get through. We should speak to Logan and Dolly Appleton first. Hopwood had singled them both out for special treatment. I didn't get much about Flora out of Ricky. He tried to make out that there was nothing special between them, but he could be covering up. Isla Prentice certainly thinks they were an item. Word soon gets round. For all we know, Dolly might lay the blame for what happened to Flora at the Hopwoods' door."

Rocco looked doubtful. "You think it was the mother that had a go at Hopwood?"

Ruth shrugged. "It's possible. She wouldn't be human if she didn't harbour a grudge. We could do with knowing a lot more about the relationship between Ricky and Flora. I'll give him a little time to get his head together, then I'll go and speak to him again."

"I spoke to Josie Wilkins when I was at the scene," Calladine told them. "I hadn't planned to, but she was out on the deck. She'd heard Hopwood scream when he was attacked." He scratched his head. "Shame it had to be her. Josie has got enough on her plate right now."

"Did she see who it was?" Nigel asked.

"No, but she did hear two men arguing. It was definitely male voices. She said nothing about any woman."

Ruth shrugged. "That puts paid to Dolly Appleton being involved, then."

"That's if we believe her," Calladine pointed out. "Thinking about the cold case, I'm not inclined to take anything Josie tells me at face value."

"Best keep an open mind. Rule nothing out." Rocco nodded sagely.

"We'll hit Heron House together," Calladine decided. "I've already got uniform going door to door. Nigel and I will find Bernie Logan." He nodded at the young DC. "Ruth, you and Rocco have a word with Dolly. Tread carefully, but see what she has by way of an alibi."

Nigel waved a handful of paper at them. "The list is huge. The whole of Heron House must be on there."

"We'll try and eliminate the obvious first," Calladine replied. "We'll start with those who haven't paid the Hopwoods anything in the last month."

He looked at the team. "While we're at it, don't forget about Flora. People might not want to say too much about the Hopwoods, so take the opportunity to ask about her, and particularly her relationship with Ricky. The clientele of the Pheasant is a good place to start. Also, just this morning forensics found hair and an earring on the ground near to where the car was parked — the one that had Flora's body in. We should know pretty soon if it's significant.

Now for the hard bit, thought Calladine. "Unfortunately the murders of Flora and Sean Hopwood aren't all we've got on our plates." He paused for a moment. "None of you will remember this case, it was a long time ago. It relates to a missing toddler, Jessica Wilkins, Josie's daughter. She was never found, either dead or alive. There were no clues, and no helpful witnesses. Someone has just handed in a jar of ashes, and a couple of items that have been identified as belonging to the child. Julian is doing DNA tests on bits of bone found amongst the ash, but it will take a while." He decided not to tell them about the bullet hole yet. "Pushed as we are, this find means we have to reopen the case. The file's on my desk. Would you make copies for everyone please, Joyce?" She nodded. "Josie Wilkins was also one of Hopwood's clients."

"Does she have a motive for killing Hopwood?" Rocco asked.

"Not that I'm aware of. Josie dealt with Hopwood the same way she dealt with everyone else she didn't like. She avoided him. If things got heated, she'd most likely set her sister Tracy on him. Nigel and I will talk to her."

Rocco was looking puzzled. "How do we tackle the cold case, sir? Who can we interview after so much time?"

"We will wait and see what forensics turn up first. The Duggan have the items from back then, and are redoing some tests. For now we have to prioritise the murders of Flora Appleton and Hopwood. I'll allocate tasks on the Wilkins case as we go along."

* * *

Ruth and Rocco drove towards the Hobfield. "Feeling better now?" Ruth asked. "The week away, has it helped you get your head together?"

"Not really. I still miss her. I don't think that will ever go away."

Ruth sighed. "It's the same for all of us, you know. Imogen was great, and we loved her, but we have to get on with it. She'd expect that, being the practical type that she was."

"Well, running away didn't help. The course was a washout. There was only me and three others on it. Two of them didn't drink and the third had brought his girlfriend along. She was staying at the pub in the village."

Ruth laughed. "Rocco, you are an idiot." She thought for a moment. "A girlfriend might do you good. You don't say much, but there must be someone, surely?"

Rocco grinned. "I have been seeing someone. She was another reason I came back. She was giving me earache."

Ruth was curious and pleasantly surprised. Rocco hardly ever talked about his private life. Ruth had met his parents on a couple of occasions, but that was it.

"Come on then — spill. Who is she?"

Rocco looked embarrassed. "You're going to think I'm mad."

"So I know her?" Ruth smiled. "Let me think. Who do I know that you'd be shy about?"

"We all know her. We've met her before, a while ago, during another investigation."

Ruth laughed. "So she's in the force! You *are* mad! You do realise that there'll be no social life. When you're working she'll be off and vice versa."

"I'm sure we'll cope. At least she knows what to expect."

"Never mind the *she*. What's her name?" Ruth couldn't understand why he was being so cagey.

Rocco shrugged. "I'll tell you later, when we're all together, back at the nick."

"Okay, if that's how you want it. Must be serious, though, if you're going to make some big announcement."

"I didn't say that. But it's best if I tell you all at once."

Ruth was really curious now. "Go on! Aren't you going to give me a clue?"

"Remember that course they sent me on a couple of months ago? She was there too and we had a few drinks.

We've been out a few times, and hardly stopped emailing and talking on the phone. The lease on her flat has just run out. I hope I'm not rushing things, but I've said she can have a room at mine."

Ruth knew that Rocco lived alone. He was an independent soul. "You've gone from having us all wondering, to a live-in lover, and none of us knew a thing." Ruth shook her head. "We're on your side, you know. We all just want you to be happy."

"I know that, Ruth. It's only been a short time, and we're still getting to know one another. It does feel right, though, us being together."

Ruth stared grimly at the road ahead. "That's how me and Jake started. Now look at us. At each other's throats mostly."

"You and Jake are sound. Anyone can see that."

Ruth shook her head. "Me and Jake are a mess. I'm beginning to think that the relationship has run its course."

Rocco stared at her. "But you've got Harry. You have to make it work."

"Rocco, you are such an innocent. Me and Harry will be fine, with or without Jake Ireson. I don't fancy it much, the single mum bit. But if needs must, I'll give it a go. One thing I do know is that I can't stand much more of the sniping that's gone on recently."

The tower block loomed ahead of them. "There it is. Heron House." Rocco shivered. "Hate the damn place."

"Still haunts you, does it?"

"Well, I'll always have the scar from where that lunatic clobbered me." Rocco rubbed at his short, dark hair.

"You had us all worried that day, especially Tom," Ruth told him.

"My parents weren't best pleased either. They went on at me for weeks to give it all up. My mum even got me an interview with the bank she works for!"

Ruth smiled. "They worry about you, Rocco. It's understandable."

"What's she like, this woman we're going to see?"

"Dolly Appleton is okay. But she is naturally hurting from losing her daughter. Flora was seeing Ricky Hopwood, but they'd fallen out apparently."

"Motive for murder?"

"I don't know. It was Sean Hopwood that got it, not Ricky. So it doesn't make much sense. Anyway, we'll speak to her, and see what we think."

Chapter 16

"She's not in, love." Annie Chadwick was out on the deck near Dolly Appleton's flat, gossiping with another woman. She flashed Ruth a brief smile.

"Any idea where she's gone?" Ruth asked.

"She's a funeral to see to."

The two detectives were about to leave when Annie called to Ruth. She held out a leaflet. "Have one of these! It's about that trip at the weekend. The one to Shrewsbury that Len told you about. We could do with bumping up the numbers. Make it worth our while getting the minibus."

"I don't think I'll be able to make it," Ruth replied, but took the flyer anyway. That was when she noticed Annie's hand. The sight of the two mangled fingers was quite shocking. "What on earth happened to you?"

"An accident, love. They did their best at the hospital but it looks like I've got an infection in them now."

"What sort of accident?" Ruth took Annie's hand and examined it. Annie had applied a makeshift dressing, but it was hanging off.

Annie grimaced. "A burn. I'm far too clumsy, that's my problem. I'll have to be more careful in future."

Ruth gently released the hand, and she and Rocco turned to leave. "I'd get that looked at as soon as, if I were you. The health centre's open. Have a word with Dr Hoyle, he'll sort you out."

They got into the lift.

"That looked really bad," said Rocco quietly.

"It didn't happen that long ago either. Funny that Frank never mentioned it." Ruth was frowning.

Rocco looked at her. "What are you thinking?"

"A burnt hand, a beaten man, plus Dolly's flat nearly gets torched. Heaven knows how many more 'accidents' folk around here have met with. I'm wondering if this has anything to do with Hopwood. Remind me when we get back to check if Annie and Frank Chadwick are on that list of Nigel's."

* * *

Calladine and Nigel Hallam found Bernie Logan at home in his flat, nursing his sore head.

He greeted them with a scowl. "What d'you want now? I've given a statement. There's nothing else I want to say."

"This isn't about the beating," Calladine told him. "You may not have heard yet but someone took a knife to Sean Hopwood. Not content with that, they shoved him over the rail of the first-floor deck."

Logan broke into a happy smile. Through swollen eyes, he looked from one detective to the other. "Dead, is he?"

"Yes." Calladine replied simply, and watched Logan's smile widen.

"I won't pretend I'm sorry, but it's got nowt to do with me, so you can get lost, copper. Shame it didn't happen sooner, then I might have been spared this little lot." Logan touched his face.

This was surprisingly candid from a man who must have realised he'd be a number-one suspect.

"What have you been up to today?" Calladine asked.

"I've been in bed all morning. Look at the state of me. Do I look like I could take on Hopwood and win? Anyway, our Kyle is asleep in the next room. He'll confirm it. Poor lad's had a long, hard night at the Pheasant. First they have a lock-in, then Wallace wants him to serve up breakfast. Our Kyle works there. I say work, but in reality he's nothing but a bloody skivvy. No good refusing. That landlord is a brute. You'll have seen his eye. Toss-up between who's worse — him or Hopwood."

Calladine looked at him. "Wallace did that? Kyle told me he got the injury knocking his head on a pan."

Logan shook his head. "You didn't believe that story any more than I did."

"So your Kyle was home by eight this morning?" Hopwood had been attacked at about nine thirty.

"He'd been in bed at least an hour by then," said Logan.

Calladine looked closer at him. "Are you sure?"

"Course I'm bloody sure!"

"When did you see Sean Hopwood last?" Calladine asked him.

Logan averted his eyes. "Yesterday afternoon when he came knocking for money. I told him straight, I've got nowt. Said I'd try to pay something next week. He seemed happy enough and buggered off."

"And he didn't come back last night, and leave you with that?" Calladine nodded at Logan's face.

"No. Like I said before, I fell."

"Anyone see that, Mr Logan?" asked Nigel.

"No, son. I fell over my big feet climbing up the steps in this pile of crap."

Calladine's mobile rang. It was Ruth. He went out onto the deck to take the call.

"Dolly has disappeared," she told him. "Of course she could be shopping or something, but it seems odd."

"I've got nothing fresh out of Logan either. Anyone talk to you?"

"Nothing useful. No one's sorry. You should see the smiles when I tell them what's happened."

Calladine went back inside. Kyle Logan had joined his father. He looked dishevelled in tracksuit bottoms, his hair messy. "You been in all day, lad?"

"I got home about eight and I've been in bed since," said Kyle.

"And your dad?"

"He's been here too. He's not right yet, needs his rest."

"If you do remember anything about your 'accident,' and want to talk, give me a ring." Calladine handed Bernie Logan a card, and they left the flat.

"What d'you think?" Nigel asked when they were outside.

"I think he got a pasting from Hopwood and is frightened to say, in case we pin the killing on him. We can't rule him out, but given the state of him, it's unlikely. It would be handy if we could find a witness to the assault who is prepared to talk."

Calladine decided to return to the Pheasant, in order to check out Kyle Logan's story.

* * *

There were just a couple of solitary drinkers in the pub.

Mark Wallace glowered at them from behind the bar. "What do you two want?"

Calladine forced a smile. "A couple more questions. The time Kyle Logan knocked off will do for starters."

"Why, what's he done?"

Calladine moved to a nearby table and sat down. Nigel remained at the bar, talking to one of the regulars.

"He reckons you had a lock-in." Calladine shouted across to the landlord.

Mark Wallace gave him a long, hard look. "My business. I had a few friends stay behind and we'd a game of cards. Nothing wrong in that."

"Back to Kyle."

Wallace stalked across and sat down at the table. "Look, copper, I don't want any aggro from you lot. Making a living in this shithole is hard enough as it is."

Calladine stared at him. "Just answer the question."

"Stupid lad fell asleep. Just before eight, I found him kipping on the sofa in the back room. I told him to go home."

"You're sure about the time?"

"Yep. The news was on the radio. They'd just done a time check."

"See how easy it is when you try?" Calladine smiled. "Did you give him the black eye?"

Wallace sat up straight. "Is that what he said? I'll bloody kill him!"

"It was his father said it actually. Well, did you?"

"No! It's not on to assault the staff. They tend to leave you in the lurch when you do that." He gave a slight chuckle.

"The car Flora was dumped in was found just over there, on that bit of spare ground." Calladine pointed to the empty space he could see through the window.

"Look, Kyle's damn eye, that girl, none of it had owt do with anyone here. We see nowt and we say nowt. Safer that way."

"What are you afraid of, Mr Wallace?" Nigel sat down at the table.

Wallace got to his feet and drew himself up to his full height. He was way over six foot and about eighteen stone.

"I'm afraid of bugger all, lad," he growled. "You'd do well to remember that, and get lost. There's nothing for you here."

Calladine and Nigel decided to take his advice.

Outside, Nigel asked, "Get anything useful, sir?"

"Bernie Logan's alibi stands up. He said he was home in bed and so was Kyle when Hopwood was stabbed. In effect, they are providing an alibi for each other."

"Do we still suspect Bernie Logan then?"

"We'll keep an open mind," Calladine replied. "We only have the Logans' word that they were both in and asleep. Kyle is hardly going to stand up against his dad, is he?"

"We're not doing very well, are we, sir?"

"No, Nigel, we're not. Apart from one dodgy alibi, we've got nothing. People won't talk. No one saw anything. No one knows anything. No one can hazard a guess at who might have wanted Hopwood dead. They're lying, the bloody lot of 'em." Calladine rubbed his head.

Chapter 17

Calladine and Nigel walked back towards Heron House. Calladine was in despair. They could knock on doors all day and night, but he knew they'd get nowhere. "We need a breakthrough, but it's going to be down to forensics."

His mobile rang.

"Inspector, would you care to come in and tell me what you're up to? Apart from Joyce, the place is empty." DCI Rhona Birch sounded distinctly annoyed.

Calladine rolled his eyes. Birch seemed to think they were all out on some jolly. "We've got a couple of murders on our hands, ma'am. Yesterday, the body of a girl was found, the lass had been killed the week before. Then a man was stabbed and killed on the Hobfield this morning. Consequently we're mob handed on the estate while it's fresh in the memory. Problem is, the dead man was universally hated, so we're getting nowhere."

"So you can spare me some time then? Come in. I could do with a word."

Three months off and still no better for it. DCI Birch was issuing orders like she'd never been away.

He turned to Nigel. "Keep at it, lad. Take one of the uniforms and continue going door to door. See what you can get. I've got to go back to the nick. Our great leader has shown her face at last."

Calladine had just got into the car when his mobile rang again. It was Julian, calling from the Duggan.

"I think I may have found something of interest," he began. "Apart from re-examining the items taken from Josie Wilkins's flat and the pushchair at the time of the child's disappearance, I am looking again at the DNA results. There is plenty of DNA belonging to Josie, Tracy and the child, but certain other items have traces of DNA from two other people. A child's beaker — one of those with a spout — has unspecified DNA on it, plus a glass that once held whiskey."

"Neither of the two women mentioned anyone else being in their flat that day. Could the samples be from some other time? The days just before the child's disappearance, for example?"

"I can't say. You will need to investigate that."

"Okay, I'll check the photos and evidence logs. Thanks for the heads up, Julian."

It was something at least. Calladine drove back to the nick, racking his brains. Why hadn't either Josie or Tracy said anything about other people? Had these others been there when Josie left for the park with Jessica? The more he raked around in this case, the more anomalies turned up.

Back in his office, Calladine retrieved the heavy file from the bottom drawer of his desk. He was concerned. Neither he nor anyone else had been curious about these items at the time, or their significance. They should have been. Then he looked at the clock. Birch wouldn't wait much longer. With a weary sigh, he left the file for later. He'd better go and get it over with.

* * *

"You're looking very well, ma'am. A tan suits you," Calladine said.

Rhona Birch had lost a bit of weight too, and her short, no-nonsense hairstyle had highlights where the sun had bleached it.

"I had plenty of time to acquire one. That stupid son of mine led me a right merry dance," she said.

"But you found him?"

She nodded.

"Safe and well?"

"He was shacked up with some slip of a girl in a remote holiday village in Queensland." She sighed heavily and shifted on her chair. "I've had to leave him behind. Had no choice. He's a big lad now, and he doesn't want to come home. He's got himself a job of sorts, and they've found somewhere to live. What can I do?" She held out her hands, palms up. "He's got a damn good degree that didn't come cheap. Now he's quite happy to throw it all away and waste his life working in some beach café!"

"You'll have seen the incident board?" Calladine changed the subject hastily. He had never been comfortable with the notion of Birch and motherhood. He just couldn't reconcile the two. "We've got a dead teenage girl, a thug of a moneylender has been killed on the Hobfield, and we've got a cold case come back to life — with complications."

"Did you know that Nigel Hallam has asked for a transfer?"

Calladine stared at her. How come she knew and he didn't? But it came as no surprise that the DC wanted to leave them. "Has he changed his mind about CID, ma'am?" From what he remembered, CID was all the young man had ever wanted. What had gone wrong?

"No. Apparently it's down to you lot."

Calladine didn't like the look she gave him one bit. Those beady eyes of hers were boring into his skull. She was looking for answers.

"The sensitive soul doesn't feel he's fitting in," Birch said at last. "He is convinced that the team resent him, that he's being left out." She paused, no doubt waiting for Calladine to protest. But how could he? Birch was right. Nigel Hallam didn't fit in.

"Did you know that one of the superintendents at Central is Hallam's uncle?"

No, he hadn't, was the short answer to that.

"He has gone blubbing to him," Birch continued. "So the super in question has had a word in my ear. He thinks the poor lad needs a second chance, somewhere different." She gave an exasperated sigh. "Since when did policing get so touchy-feely? I'm at a loss, I really am. In my opinion, he hasn't given it long enough, and I told him so. But it did no good. He wants to go as soon as possible"

Calladine had picked up on none of this. He knew the team were a tad cagey around Nigel, and he had his own reservations about him. But all that could change, given time. They just needed to see what the lad was made of.

"He has replaced Imogen, ma'am. Surely he's not stupid. He's got to be aware of how we all feel about her. But that doesn't mean we dislike *him*. We simply don't know him well enough. That will come when we've worked together a little longer. I keep hoping that sooner or later, he'll gel."

"Well, I don't think he will. We're flogging a dead horse with this one. His transfer has been confirmed. Nigel Hallam is going to join Central as from Monday next."

"So what do we do, ma'am? We're a man down and busy. We need a replacement, and quick."

"There is someone earmarked for your team. She recently joined CID after doing two years with uniform in Sheffield. She graduated from Manchester University with a very good degree in criminology."

Calladine rolled his eyes. "Graduate entry. I suppose she expects to be chief constable within a decade. What's she like? I imagine she thinks she knows it all, having a degree and all that."

"I met her once. She struck me as being the straightforward type. She fully intends to settle in Leesdon, and to give the job her all."

"Do we have a name?"

"Sorry, I don't have the paperwork to hand. But she's an intense young woman with a sharp, analytical mind. She's tipped to go far. Make her welcome. And please try a little harder with this one. We don't want to get a reputation, do we?"

"Of course not, ma'am. When does she arrive?"

"The day after tomorrow. Make good use of her, Calladine. Let's see some progress on the cases you're working on."

* * *

Everyone was still out, gathering information on the Hobfield. Apart from Joyce, who was hammering away on her keyboard, the incident room was empty. Calladine sat quietly in his office with the Jessica Wilkins file. He needed to think.

Julian had said to look at the photos. Those showing the inside of the flat had been enlarged, and he could clearly see a draining board stacked with washed pots in the kitchen. The items Julian had mentioned were on a small coffee table in the sitting room. The feeding bottle and mug belonging to Jessica and Josie, plus the beaker and glass that Julian was now examining. Calladine turned back to the draining board and the pile of clean pots. It looked like four people had had a drink that day, prior to leaving the house and after Josie had washed up.

He scanned through the report. After Jessica went missing, a woman police officer had taken Josie straight to the station from the park. She was very distressed. They had rung Tracy on her mobile and asked her to come to the station. The flat was then searched. The PC had sat with both Josie and Tracy at the station while they were questioned. That meant no one had gone back to the flat. It was exactly as Josie had left it to take Jessica to the park.

In that case, Josie must have had visitors earlier on. A child and an adult. The child had drunk juice or milk, and the adult had had a whiskey. So who were they? And why hadn't either Josie or Tracy said anything about them? Tracy had stated that she'd been at work, so she couldn't have known who had called at Josie's flat.

The other odd thing in the statement was that Josie had insisted she'd taken Jessica to the park because she was fed up with being in by herself. It was a nice day, and she fancied some company, a chat with the other mums. That meant her statement was at odds with the cups on the table. Plus, as the witnesses had said, Josie hadn't spoken to anyone that afternoon. Far from chatting to the other people in the park, she'd sat alone, reading a magazine. So why lie? What had she been trying to hide, and why wasn't she questioned about her behaviour? Even Calladine hadn't seen any significance in this contradiction back then.

He picked up the phone and rang Julian. "You're right," he began. "And I think what you've spotted is important. What I don't understand is why no one pieced this together back then. The photos are clear enough, and the items on that coffee table are listed as being bagged and taken. Why weren't questions asked?"

"DNA tests were done on them, but no matches were found. The items were not seen as significant, Tom. Remember, the team were looking for the person who'd kidnapped the child from the *park*. You had no reason to suspect that anything untoward had happened in that flat."

"You're right, Julian. But perhaps the questions should have been asked, if only in the interests of being thorough. We are only interested now because of what has been found — the ashes, slide and blanket. Plus, how the little girl was killed. It all happened before Ruth's time. She is a fresh pair of eyes and has already spotted several anomalies. I think she could have something. No one actually saw Jessica in her pushchair that day. This case may not be a straightforward snatch — if there is such a thing."

"I plan to run the DNA taken from those items through the database again," Julian said. "With luck, it might tell you who else was in the flat that day."

"I suppose I could just ask Josie?" Calladine said.

"You could, but if something untoward did happen she is unlikely to be helpful."

"And if there's no match on the database?"

"Then you can ask."

Calladine was thinking hard. "There might be a perfectly simple explanation. A neighbour or a friend brings a child round, the kids play, then the grownups have a drink before they leave."

"And Josie Wilkins dishes out whiskey? In the middle of the afternoon?" Julian sounded scornful.

Calladine rubbed his head. "This has got me curious and no mistake. Thanks, Julian. I'll get back to you."

On its own the possibility that Josie might have had visitors in her flat that afternoon was innocent enough. But why not say so? Was she hiding a huge secret about what had actually happened to little Jessica?

Chapter 18

Dolly couldn't leave things as they were. It had happened in the block she lived in. For all she knew, the others would think *she* was responsible for what happened to Hopwood. Gossip was rife. Some said he'd been stabbed. But he'd also fallen or been pushed from the first floor to the ground below. That was no accident. Someone had wanted to make sure. Had it been one of the group? Dolly had to speak to the others, find out what they knew. Once she'd calmed down, she made her way to Frank's allotment. At this time of year, he was always there during the hours of daylight. She needed to discuss what had happened to Hopwood.

The Leesdon allotments were on a tract of land to one side of Leesdon Park. There were dozens of them. The entire area was dotted with sheds and small picket fences. Where to start?

She made her way up the main path. "Who d'you want?" shouted a man digging amidst his potatoes.

"Frank Chadwick," she replied.

He pointed into the distance. "Far end, love. Can't miss it. The one with the greenhouse that's got no glass."

Had Frank heard? Dolly wondered. Hopwood's murder hadn't even made the local news yet. Dolly tramped between the fences, trying to work things out. Had one of the group taken it upon themselves to solve the problem of Hopwood? She hoped not. If that was the case, they would have to meet again to sort out the alibis the nurse had talked about.

All of them were on Hopwood's 'hot' list. If the police did get wind of the meeting, they'd have to all tell the same story. The police would be told they'd met to discuss their common problem, that of the debt they owed to the Hopwoods. Once Frank knew, he'd tell the others, and anything incriminating would be removed from the locker. Then, all would be as it should, and no one would be any the wiser.

* * *

Frank Chadwick could see Dolly coming up the hill towards him and his heart sank. He needed some time alone. He was out of breath, sitting on a chair in the doorway of his shed, gasping.

"Dolly! You shouldn't be here," he wheezed.

"Have you heard? Someone's killed Hopwood."

Frank looked at her and shook his head. "Comes as no surprise." He clutched at his chest.

His face crumpled with pain each time he inhaled. "Are you alright, Frank? You don't look well."

He shook his head. "Too much rushing around this morning. I'm not supposed to overdo things. COPD, you know."

Frank liked Dolly, and was usually happy to chat. But not today. He smiled apologetically. "You should go. I'll be off home myself if this chest of mine doesn't ease."

"What have you been up to?"

Frank didn't want her concern. He just wanted to be left alone. "Nothing, Dolly. I overdid it getting here, that's all. It's a nice day. I walked the long way round and got a bit puffed."

Dolly had never seen him like this before. She knew he had bad lungs. As a kid he'd worked in the local cotton factory. A lot of people around here had lung problems because of that. Back then, no one worried about the dust. "What are we going to do about Hopwood? The police are bound to question us."

Frank heaved a painful sigh and shook his head. He had a glass of water at his side and he took a sip. Any other time he'd have been happy to talk to Dolly, flattered that she'd sought him out. She was in her late forties, attractive, with dark hair and a slim figure. Every Saturday night she'd get done up to the nines, then her and a friend would spend the night down at the social club. Dolly was popular, well liked. Frank was surprised she'd never got herself a decent man. Flora's father hadn't hung around for long after she'd been born. Since Flora's murder though, she was very different. No make-up, her hair was a mess, and her clothes looked as if they'd been slept in. It was a shame, not like her, but he understood why. Dolly was devastated by what had happened to her daughter. She could no longer cope. If the woman didn't get her act together soon, Frank doubted they'd ever see the old Dolly again.

"He's been murdered, Frank. Don't you understand?" Dolly hissed. "Someone stabbed Hopwood, then pushed him off the first floor of the flats this morning."

Unable to speak, Frank waved his hand at her.

"Was it you? Did you decide to go it alone?"

"What makes you think that?" This brought on another fit of coughing. After a while, he said, "I was all for going with that nurse's idea. Drugging the bastard."

Dolly stared at him. "I've not seen you like this before, Frank. It's more than your chest. You're acting strange."

"My old problem. I'm out of breath, that's all it is."

Dolly didn't believe him. Something wasn't right with Frank, but he obviously didn't want to discuss it.

"I'm worried, Frank. The police are bound to come round to mine. They know how much I hated the man. After the fire incident, I'll be top of the list."

"You're getting ahead of yourself, Dolly. Bernie has that spot." Frank grimaced. "Hopwood gave him that beating. Bernie told them he didn't know who it was, but the police aren't daft. They know what's what."

"Do you think Bernie did it? He does have a temper on him. Every bit as bad as Hopwood's when he's pushed."

Frank nodded. "It could have been. But whoever it was, we have to keep quiet."

"I'll crack under pressure, I know I will. I'm eaten up with worry. I've got to sort Flora's funeral. It's all too much, and now on top of that, this has happened."

Frank shook his head. "You have to calm down, woman! The police have nothing. The group — you, we, have done nothing wrong. We met and we talked, that's all. In the unlikely event you are asked about the meeting, you tell them you were nowhere near. The nurse will back you up. You can say you were talking to him."

"But I wasn't! I'd just got back from being with you lot. It was about nine in the morning when I got home. It must have been within thirty minutes or so of Hopwood being attacked. I could have been seen. Anyone might come forward, make me out to be a liar."

"When the police talk to you, stay calm. No one saw us. It was too early. Like we agreed, just tell the police you were talking to the nurse about Flora."

* * *

Calladine was about to join the others on the Hobfield when his mobile rang. It was his daughter, Zoe.

She spoke quietly. "Would you pop in and see me? I don't want to talk on the phone. What I have to say is . . . delicate."

Another one. First Julian and now Zo. "What's wrong?" Calladine didn't like mysteries if they concerned his daughter.

"I'll explain when you get here." He heard the tension in her voice. "It's a difficult one, but it's something you need to know right now."

"Okay, love. Put the kettle on and I'll be round in five."

Calladine's daughter was a solicitor with an office on the High Street above the estate agents owned by her partner, Jo Brandon. As well as setting up home together, the two young women had formed a successful business partnership. Between them, they handled most of the house sales in Leesworth.

Calladine left the station, walked across the car park, and out the back way into Leesdon centre. It was late afternoon. The shops were still busy, and the sun was out again. It gave the small town a pleasant lift.

Zoe and Jo were deep in conversation when he arrived. A couple were chatting animatedly by the property boards. The minute he came in the door, Zoe gestured for him to follow her into the back.

"I didn't know what to do, but I can't just sit on it. If Ruth finds out, she'll kill me."

"Ruth? What's going on?" Calladine was really curious now.

"First thing this morning, before we were even open, Jake Ireson knocked on the door. He was on his way into school." Zoe paused and folded her arms. "I feel like I'm telling tales, but I can't just do nothing." She gave her father a long, hard look. "He spoke to Jo, but I was also here. He asked me not to say anything." Zoe ran a hand through her short black hair.

"Spit it out, girl! Whatever it is, it's obviously doing your head in."

"Jake wants Jo to do a valuation on their house." She waited for a response. "You know," she prompted, "on his and Ruth's house. A valuation with a view to selling!"

"Jake is thinking of moving?"

"Well, he must be. But they've only had that house two minutes. He told Jo it had to be done quickly, and asked how long it would take to sell."

"Does Ruth know?"

"Has she said anything to you?"

"Not a word."

"Then I reckon she doesn't." Zoe gnawed on her bottom lip. "What's going on, Dad? Are they having problems?"

"Ruth has spoken a bit about the state of play in that relationship, and it's not good. Like you, I don't like speaking about her behind her back, but things must be worse than she made out."

"Jake's got some nerve!"

"Ruth isn't happy with the way things are. But it's hard, bringing up a child and working flat out. They are bound to have the odd rough patch."

"This isn't a rough patch, Dad. He wants to sell up. I asked him if he wanted to buy something else but he said not. He could be planning to sell, split the proceeds and go their own separate ways."

Calladine's heart sank. "Ruth would be devastated if that happened. I'm sure their current problems are just that — current. Once Harry gets a bit older, things will be better. Living together, having a child, it's a lot to cope with for two people used to doing their own thing for so long. Ruth loves Jake, I know she does. I think the pair of them could do with a break."

"Given that isn't going to happen any time soon, what are you going to do?"

"God knows. I'll have to tell her, I suppose." He looked at Zoe, hoping she might offer some alternative bright idea. This was relationship stuff, something he was notoriously bad at. "Perhaps I'd be better leaving it up to Jake."

"You can't do that! Once Ruth knows Jake has been here, she'll realise that you must know. Tell her, Dad. It's her home too. Stop wimping about."

"Okay, love, I'll do it. I'll offer a shoulder to cry on, and if she wants, a couple of rooms in my house."

Zoe stroked his arm and smiled. "That is if he is planning to do one. Tread carefully. Don't say too much, and don't take sides. With any luck, they might put things right."

Good advice from Zoe, as always. He smiled. She was very like him. The same dark hair, the slim build he'd had when he was younger, and the regular features that made Zoe a very pretty young woman. He'd missed being there when she was growing up, and he regretted that. But there was nothing he could do about it. Until she moved north and found him, he'd had no idea that Zoe even existed.

"As if I didn't have enough to think about."

"Difficult case?"

"Aren't they always?" He grimaced. "I'd better get off."

"Get round to ours for your tea one night this week. Jo will make something special."

He kissed her cheek. "Thanks. I'll let you know."

* * *

Back at the nick, Calladine was relieved to see that Ruth and the others were still out working the Hobfield. God knows what he was going to say to her. He couldn't work out what Jake was up to. Why had he not told Ruth that he'd booked a valuation? What was he up to?

Worrying about what Zoe had said was playing havoc with his concentration. Calladine had no choice. He'd have to speak to Ruth as soon as possible.

He rang her. "I could do with a word in private. It's a personal matter. Give it half an hour then meet me at the café in the library, and don't bring any of the others with you."

Chapter 19

"Do you remember Roly, the homeless bloke who turns up around here every so often?" Ruth put her coat and bag over the back of a chair. "Well, he's back. Unknown to anyone who matters, he's been dossing down under the canal bridge by the viaduct. He wandered onto the Hobfield earlier, looking for a handout from the community centre and got a rollicking from uniform. Old and unwashed he might be, but Roly is still as sharp as ever. I'll have a word later, see if he's seen or heard anything."

Calladine wasn't listening, his mind was on how to begin this conversation.

"What's up, Tom? You've got a face like a slapped backside." Ruth sat down and took a sip of the coffee he'd ordered for her. "Perfect," she said, and grabbed a biscuit. "Roly is worth talking to. Can't say we got much else. Banged on a lot of doors and ended up with nothing but sore hands. Nothing on Hopwood and even less on Flora Appleton. Finding the weapon would help, but how likely is that?"

"This is a thankless task. No one will talk to us. Once word gets round that Hopwood is dead, it'll get even worse," Calladine said.

"One thing I have detected: the atmosphere around the estate has changed. Everyone is happy. Obviously, we found no one who's sorry about what's happened."

"Forget that for the minute. I want to talk about something else." He had to get this over with.

"Serious, is it? You look fed up."

"I've heard something. I've been going over it, wondering whether to tell you or not, but you need to know." He paused, looking at her puzzled face. "So I'm just going to say it — okay?" He took a breath. "Jake went into Jo's estate agents this morning and booked a valuation on your house."

Ruth stared at him. "Are you sure?"

He knew his face said it all.

"Of course you are. Zoe told you. Bet she rang you special. Why did she not just tell me?" Now she was annoyed.

"Because she was worried. She didn't know what it meant. Jake wasn't interested in looking at other properties to buy and he didn't explain himself either."

"Typical Jake! He's a bloody fool. He must have realised I'd find out. Apart from which, we jointly own that house. So he can't put it in the hands of an agent without my signature on a document." Ruth slammed her cup back onto the saucer, slopping coffee onto the table. "What the hell is he playing at? The idiot has said nothing to me."

"Could there be an explanation? Is it a surprise perhaps?"

"Oh, it's that alright! I'll bloody surprise him when I get hold of the fool! He knows how I feel. I've no intention of moving again for a while. If we move now, we won't break even. Moving to the house we're in now has cost us a fortune. What the hell is going on inside that head of his?"

"I'm sorry, Ruth."

"It's not your fault. It's my problem. I'll stick it at the top of the list and move on."

"Has this anything to do with you two not getting on of late?" he asked.

"How the hell should I know? Jake doesn't speak to me. He grunts a lot, and flounces off to the bedroom to work. But adult conversation — no." Ruth shook her head. "I get more sense out of Harry!"

As he'd expected, Ruth had taken it badly. He felt rotten for being the one to tell her. He gave her a tentative smile. "The offer of the rooms is still open. But see if you can't sort things before you do anything rash."

* * *

They returned to the station, where Calladine called everyone to the incident room for a meeting. It was time to take stock. "Did we get *anything* from today, no matter how small?"

Rocco and Nigel conferred quietly together, amidst a general shaking of heads. "No one would say a word," Rocco confirmed. "Everyone reckoned whoever did it deserved a medal."

"Flora Appleton and Hopwood were both stabbed. Are we looking at a link?" Ruth asked.

Calladine shrugged. "I'm still not sure. There could be one. Dolly was one of the Hopwoods' clients, and Flora had been seeing Ricky."

"And they'd had a falling out — that is if we go with the gossip," Ruth added. "We haven't spoken properly to Ricky about Flora yet. We need to do that, soon as. He'll need treating gently. That young man will be very cut up over what happened."

"The CSIs are still going over that deck. They might come up with something," Nigel added.

"The Hopwood stabbing happened early, but it was daylight. Folk will have been up and about. I know most of the Hobfield residents are out of work, but they walk the dog, nip out for the morning paper. I can't believe no one saw anything at all."

Ruth shook her head. "Nevertheless, guv, we're bashing our heads against a brick wall. Even with Sean dead, they still have Ricky to contend with. He is an unknown as yet. But he could turn out to be every bit as bad as his brother. Our best bets are Bernie Logan and Dolly Appleton. They both argued with Hopwood the day before. Remember, Logan got a beating. He isn't one to let things go. He has a reputation in his own right. He'll have wanted to get even. His alibi is dodgy too. He reckons Kyle was at home asleep, like him."

Rocco looked dubious. "I don't see what Bernie Logan would have against Flora. He hated Sean Hopwood, but Flora was just a teenage girl."

Ruth nodded. "We need to know much more about that young woman's life. We might get somewhere when forensics have finished analysing the samples from the PM."

Calladine made a decision. "Okay. Given we've nothing else, we'll lean on them a little. We'll bring Bernie Logan and Ricky in for a chat. It would do no harm to speak to those three lads who found the body again, and the Prentice girl."

"I'm going to get off," Ruth told Calladine. "I can't get my brain in gear since you told me that stuff."

Calladine made for the privacy of his office, with Ruth at his heels. The others watched them go, exchanged looks and shrugged. Joyce followed their exit with the eyes of a hawk.

"It'd do you no harm to pack up early too." Ruth surveyed his cluttered desk.

"I want to look through this little lot first." He pointed to the Jessica Wilkins file. "I think things were missed in the original investigation. We were all so sure the child had been taken from the park that we never considered anything else." He paused, frowning. "We should have. I think you may be right, Ruth. Jessica might never have been in Leesdon Park that day. Maybe it was all some elaborate ruse to make everyone believe she was."

"So what does that mean? What happened to her?"

"I've no idea. But we know she was shot in the head. Of course, we don't know where that happened."

"How do you prove something like that?"

He sighed. "I'm not sure we can. Julian is looking at the forensics from the time. There were some glasses on the table, and a beaker. One was Josie's and the beaker belonged to Jessica, but we have no idea about the other two. What that and the photos seem to suggest is that there were two other people in Josie's flat that afternoon. Two people neither she nor her sister has ever told us about."

Chapter 20

Ricky Hopwood was lost without his brother. Sean might have been a difficult bastard to live with but at least he'd known how to operate the business. The punters were afraid of him. If they didn't cough up, Sean would lean hard. That soon sorted things.

Ricky looked at his reflection in the huge mirror in the hallway. He didn't look in the least bit intimidating. He was too young, too *pretty*, as Sean used to scoff. No one on that damned estate was going to take him seriously. The punters would walk all over him. They'd take liberties they'd never have dared to with Sean. A show of strength was called for, or this was the end of the moneylending business.

But what could he do? Sean had never trusted him with the heavy stuff. The trouble with Ricky was that he tended to lose it. He had a quick temper and a low boredom threshold, so he made mistakes.

As Sean often said, Ricky wasn't fit for anything but working in his brother's shadow. Despite all the money lavished on his education, Ricky had done nothing at school. He'd skipped off more times than he'd attended.

He had no idea about the business or the family finances. He didn't even know if the house was still mortgaged. If it was, how was he supposed to pay for that? He'd looked at the recent bank statements from the business. The accounts were in the black — just. Ricky knew that Sean used to salt money away, but he'd no idea where. It could be buried in the garden for all he knew. Sean would never tell him. He reckoned Ricky was rubbish with money and always kept him short.

With little else to do for the next couple of hours, Ricky turned the house upside down, but found nothing of any real value. Sean had told him they had money — so where the hell was it? Sean couldn't tell him now, but there was someone who might know. Ricky picked up the phone and rang Adrian Hampson, his brother's solicitor. They had met frequently over the years. Whenever Adrian came to the house the two of them would be closeted away for hours. Sean always refused to tell Ricky what they'd discussed. Hampson had to know something. He was the last resort.

"I'm very sorry, Ricky. I haven't seen Sean in a while. I had no idea he was so ill."

"He wasn't. Some bastard took a knife to him."

He heard the solicitor cough.

"The police are investigating, I take it?"

"God knows! No one cares. No one liked Sean, did they? He was hard on folk, used his fists too much."

"So how can I help?"

"It's very simple. With Sean dead, I need money to keep this place and the business going. We are moneylenders after all," Ricky added with a humourless laugh. "Sean said there was plenty. Well, it's not in the bank, so where is it?"

"I have a copy of Sean's will in the office. I'll have a look at it and get back to you."

But Ricky couldn't wait. He was fast running out of patience. "Haven't you been listening? I need money now.

I'm the only family Sean had, so it's all bound to come to me. What do I tell the punters who want a loan? I haven't got a penny! Do you imagine Sean wanted the business to go bust within days of his death? Because that's what'll happen if I don't get the funds to carry on."

Silence.

Eventually the solicitor said, "Okay, I understand your predicament. And you are right. As I recall, under the terms of Sean's will you are the sole beneficiary. Do you have a death certificate yet?"

"No. He only died today. Try somewhere called the Duggan if you need to ask what happened. I can't wait for days while things get sorted. I need money straight away. For reasons best known to himself, Sean kept me practically penniless, and he told me nowt about how much we had."

"Typical Sean. But rest assured, there is money."

Ricky was getting angry. "So where is it? I need you to come here! Today. I want to know where the money is and how I get my hands on it."

"Calm down. Plans were made. I have a letter for you. Sean left it with me many years ago. I was instructed to give it to you in the event of his death. If everything is as you describe, then under the circumstances there should not be a problem."

"Make it quick," Ricky instructed. "None of the usual drawn-out stuff you solicitors are fond of. If I don't get some money soon, there will be nothing left of the business. Want to be responsible for that one?"

"The letter I have in safekeeping will hold all the information you need, I'm sure."

"When can I get hold of this letter?"

"Actually there is a letter and a small suitcase. I will drop both off at your house this evening."

Ricky smiled. Sean could have been secreting his money away for years. That had to be what was the letter was about. It'd tell him where it was. He ended the call to

Hampson and sat in Sean's armchair. He leaned back, into the comforting smell of Sean's aftershave. It made him feel safe. But he'd have to face up to it. Sean wasn't coming home again. Ricky was going to have to learn how to cope on his own, and fast. Getting his hands on the money was just the first step.

Chapter 21

Ruth walked through the front door and threw her bag onto a chair. Jake leapt to his feet, as if he'd been waiting for her. "I've sorted tea," he said. "Day go alright? Not too stressful?"

"Bloody awful just about sums it up. We've got a murder, a stabbing that's now turned into a second murder, and a cold case on the go." She followed him into the kitchen. "What have you done with Harry? You haven't forgotten to pick him up, have you?"

Jake shook his head. "No, he's with Mrs Potter next door. I wanted to talk to you."

Jake was smiling, which made Ruth both angry and suspicious. Gone was the moody bloke with the attitude. In his place was this jolly soul who had everything organised. There was not a school exercise book to be seen.

Ruth sighed inwardly. It had been good while it lasted, now for the fireworks. "Calladine told me something today. You went into the estate agents this morning. You want a valuation done on our house." She stood with her arms folded and glared at him. He seemed to be searching for words. This could be bad.

"Come and sit down," he said eventually.

Ruth followed him to the sofa and sat down beside him. She'd no idea what was coming, and it made her nervous. He took a glossy brochure from the table and started to fiddle with it.

"I don't want to move, Jake. If that's about a new estate going up somewhere, I'm not interested."

"It isn't," he said simply. "It's about a private school in Dorset." He handed her the leaflet and pointed to the photo on the front. "You must agree, it's a beautiful place."

Indeed it was. A huge stone building surrounded by grass and trees. She flipped through the pages. The school had a swimming pool, a state-of-the-art gym, everything all those bright young things aiming for university would possibly need to get them there.

"They have offered me a job. Head of English. My salary would be another fifty per cent on top of what I earn now, and that's just to start with."

Ruth was gobsmacked. This was the last thing she'd expected. She looked at him wide-eyed, filled with a mixture of shock and amazement. He must have seen the vacancy, applied, even been interviewed, and she'd had no idea.

"You're serious, aren't you?" She shook the brochure in front of his face. "You went behind my back. You expect us all to move away so that *you* can further *your* career. What about my career, Jake? Doesn't that count for anything? You've got some nerve! This is a huge step. You should have said something, at least run the idea past me first."

"I thought you'd be pleased. It's a real opportunity, a step up. We can buy another house, a better one. Initially we can have one of the cottages in the grounds. Look at the back pages. The school is slap bang in the middle of beautiful countryside. It would be great for Harry."

Ruth's head was spinning. She was exhausted enough already. There was no way she could give any of this serious thought just now. Her immediate instinct was to put her foot down. "No! It's not happening. Me and Harry are staying put." She brought her face close to his. "I have a job too, Jake. Or perhaps you don't think what I do is of any importance?"

"Of course I take your work seriously, but you can transfer. Someone with your skills and record, any police force would be glad of you."

"It's not that simple." She took his hand and looked into his eyes. "I like it where I am. I belong here, in Leesdon. I work with people I understand and like. That doesn't just happen anywhere, Jake."

He said nothing. His eyes remained glued to the brochure on his lap. Ruth nudged him but got no response. Surely he hadn't expected a different reaction from her? She began to wonder if he knew her at all. Did he even know how much her job meant to her? Plus the fact that Ruth had never lived anywhere else, or wanted to. It was a wrench too far.

* * *

Adrian Hampson handed Ricky a large manila envelope and a small suitcase. "My instructions were precise. I was to give you these items and then leave. Not how these things are usually done, but your brother was an odd one. Obviously there are things here Sean doesn't want me to see."

The solicitor brushed an imaginary piece of lint from his expensive suit and smiled at the young man. "I'm well aware that Sean didn't always stay on the right side of the law, so that," he nodded at the suitcase, "could contain anything. If there is something you don't understand, then contact me."

Ricky was puzzled. Why hadn't his brother explained how things would work once he was out of the game? Money was money, right? So why all the mystery? "I just hope there's some dosh at the end of all this. I've got bills to pay."

"I'm sure Sean will have left you amply looked after. Anything you need, Ricky, just ring me. My condolences on your loss." Adrian Hampson was already backing away. He handed Ricky a document to sign, then let himself out.

The envelope looked new. Hampson had obviously taken it from Sean and put it straight into the safe. The suitcase, however, was another matter. It was old, dating perhaps from the forties or fifties, and covered in a layer of grime. It was made of leather, and had an ivory handle. More to the point, it was locked. Ricky shook the envelope. It rattled. The key must be inside.

Ricky ripped open the envelope, put the paperwork aside and took out a small key. Moments later he was gazing at the contents of the suitcase. It made no sense. Inside, were hundreds of photographs. Some were very old, in black and white. Some were more recent, showing Ricky as a child. He picked up a few and took a closer look. There he was, a small boy playing with other children. There were also a number of documents that looked about the same age as the suitcase. Ricky took one and peered at it. It was the deeds to a house in Leesdon. He shuffled through the rest. There had to be at least another eight or nine sets of deeds in the suitcase. Sean must have been buying property for years. Why hadn't he said anything? He read through them quickly, and saw that they were all in good areas. These documents represented a small fortune in property.

Chapter 22

Wednesday

Bernie Logan and Dolly Appleton were brought into the station first thing. Bernie didn't seem bothered. Left to wait in the interview room with only a uniformed officer for company, he leaned back in his chair, folded his arms and began to mouth off at the poor copper assigned to watch him.

Dolly, on the other hand, was as nervous as a kitten. In another room down the corridor she was given tea, but her hand shook so much she spilled it. She put the cup in the saucer, tea undrunk.

"You seem troubled, Dolly," said Ruth.

"I don't know what I'm doing here. I've done nothing wrong. You know about my Flora. I've not slept for days worrying about what happened to her. How do you imagine I feel about being dragged in here at the crack of dawn? Folk will think I've done something awful."

Ruth gave a faint smile. "Tell me about your relationship with Sean Hopwood."

"I hated him, like most folk I know. But I didn't kill him," Dolly said vehemently.

"You owed him money and you couldn't pay. What did he have to say about that?"

Dolly started to speak but Ruth was only half listening. She couldn't concentrate. Her mind kept drifting back to the row she'd had with Jake last night. He refused to see her side of things. He couldn't understand why she didn't want to go with him. All he could see was the opportunity to enhance his own career. Even after hours of arguing, followed by a night spent in separate beds, nothing was sorted.

Dolly droned on. "Me and most of the estate hated the man, love. He sends that brother of his round knocking on doors. Don't pay up and Sean comes back once it's dark. We know the score, so we don't answer."

Ruth shook herself. She needed to listen. "He didn't just knock this time though, did he, Dolly? He tried to burn you out."

Dolly started weeping. "Far too fond of fire that bloody animal was. He deserved all he got."

"What do you mean — too fond of fire?"

"Nothing, slip of the tongue."

"No it wasn't. What were you getting at? Does this have anything to do with Annie Chadwick's hand?" Suddenly Ruth made the connection.

Dolly burst into tears. "He was an animal."

"I've seen the burn. Are you saying that Hopwood did that?"

Dolly nodded and bit her lip. Ruth could see she wanted to say more.

"Hopwood can't hurt you anymore, Dolly. Tell me what you know."

Dolly spoke between sobs. "He held her hand over the flame on the gas hob. He hurt her bad. Her husband says she'll not get the full use of her fingers back."

So the Chadwicks were clients of the Hopwoods too. "Why didn't they report it?" Ruth was astonished. The poor woman must have been in agony. If she'd come to them they would have arrested Hopwood straight away.

"They were frightened. We all were. Stand up against him, argue the toss and you know what happens. There's only one way to stop a man like Hopwood. I'm glad someone else did for him. Saved us the bother."

"What do you mean, Dolly? Saved you the bother?"

At this, Dolly began to cry in earnest. She wailed, "I said I wouldn't be any good! I can't pretend anymore. We all wanted him dead. Every last one of us! Logan, the Chadwicks and the others. We would have done it too, if someone hadn't got there first."

Ruth frowned. "Let me get this right, Dolly. You are telling me that you and other customers of Hopwood's were plotting kill him?"

Dolly nodded, her eyes on the floor.

"Did you attack him, Dolly?"

She shook her head.

"Do you know who did?"

Dolly's eyes darted around the room, as if she were looking for an escape route. "It couldn't have been one of us. We didn't have the time. We hadn't decided how to do it either. If you don't believe me, ask Frank."

"Frank Chadwick?"

Dolly sighed. "We had a meeting, early yesterday morning. We discussed ways of getting rid of Hopwood, but we didn't have time to do anything. Nothing was decided. So someone else must have got there first." She looked at Ruth. "I didn't kill Sean Hopwood, and I don't know who did. It could have been anyone off that estate. We all hated him."

"That's some admission you've just made, Dolly. You're telling me that you and others off the Hobfield met to discuss bumping off Sean Hopwood?" Ruth couldn't believe it. "You, the Chadwicks, Logan and others, you say?"

"I don't know them all," Dolly said. "Well, maybe by sight."

"You will have to give me their names. You see, Dolly, it's all very well for you to tell me that none of you did it, but you can't be sure, can you?"

"A nurse from the health centre, the one who runs the diabetic clinic. He was there. He'll tell you who the others were."

This complicated things even further. They would have no option but to take Dolly and the Chadwicks to task for even considering murder, even if the intended victim was a violent bully. It didn't seem fair, but Ruth had no choice but to tell Calladine about it.

"And Flora?" Ruth asked.

Dolly shook her head. "She had nothing to do with Hopwood."

"She knew Ricky," said Ruth.

"My Flora knew all the lads. At one time she was keen on that Kyle Logan. He's another waste of space. Too fond of using his fists."

Ruth stood up. "Okay, Dolly, that'll do for now."

Ruth passed Rocco in the corridor. "What's up?" he asked.

"Is Tom with Logan?" Ruth said.

"Yes, the boss and Nigel Hallam have him in there." Rocco nodded at the interview room door.

Ruth knocked and went in. "Can I have a word?"

* * *

Calladine followed her out into the corridor.

"I've just interviewed Dolly Appleton and she told me that several of Hopwood's clients met Tuesday morning to discuss doing him in." She waited for Calladine to say something.

"Who exactly?"

"Dolly, Bernie Logan, Frank Chadwick, a nurse, John Barnett, from the health centre and a couple of others. Dolly assures me that they simply talked about it. Nothing was settled and it was only later that she heard Hopwood had been killed."

Calladine scratched his head. "Unlikely set of killers. Apart from Logan, that is."

"Even so, he's not stupid. He would know very well where suspicion is likely to fall. Mind you, it does scupper their alibis. Bernie was at this meeting, so both of them were lying to us."

"We'll be speaking to them again."

Ruth leant back against the wall. "I need some time out of the station. My mind keeps wandering. I keep losing concentration. I was daydreaming in there with Dolly, until she woke me up with her revelation. To be honest, Tom, I'm a mess. I've hardly slept and I can't get what Jake's up to out of my head."

"So you spoke to him then. What has he done?"

"No half measures this time." Ruth gave a humourless laugh. "He's gone and got some poncy job down south. He wants us all to move. No discussion, no warning. He even went to the interview without saying a thing to me."

Calladine felt his stomach lurch. "You're not thinking of going with him?" The prospect of doing this job without Ruth at his side was unbearable. What was he saying? Of course she'd have to consider it. They were a couple, they had a child, and she loved Jake.

"I don't know what to do. I don't want to go . . ."

There it was, he could hear it in her voice. She might not want this, but for the sake of her relationship with Jake, she was already giving it some thought.

Ruth shook her head. "I'd be like a fish out of water."

"Do you want to take some time off?"

"No, I've finished with Dolly. If it means anything, I don't think she killed Hopwood. She doesn't have it in her. But she did tell me that it was Hopwood who hurt Annie

Chadwick's hand. He deliberately burnt it, Tom. The vile beast!"

"I wonder how many more like her will come forward, now he's gone."

Ruth nodded. "We should speak to Annie. At least get a statement from her."

Calladine looked thoughtful. "It does give the Chadwicks a motive."

"A chat first, and we'll go from there," Ruth told him. "I can't see either of the Chadwicks being capable of killing anyone, even Hopwood. I've left Dolly in the interview room. I've no idea what to do with her. In the meantime, I thought I'd take a uniform and go and speak to Ricky. Get some fresh air."

"Take Rocco instead," Calladine told her. "Natasha is doing the PM on Hopwood this afternoon, about two. Take your time. I'll go to the Duggan with Nigel."

* * *

Ricky Hopwood greeted them with a scowl. "Found out who killed Sean yet?"

Ruth didn't smile. "We're working on it. But this isn't to do with your brother. We'd like a word with you about Flora."

He led the way into the sitting room, which had documents and photos spread over every surface, including the floor.

Ruth picked one up. "Family?"

"Some of them are me when I was a kid, the others — no idea. They could be anyone for all I know."

Ruth picked up an old colour photo. She showed it to him. "The boy in this looks like Sean. The older couple could be your grandparents."

Ricky shrugged. "Could be. I never met them. My parents were dead by the time I was three, my grandparents too. It was Sean who raised me. He left me this lot, so he must have thought they were important. Can't think why. He never talked about our family."

Ruth felt sorry for the young man. Sean Hopwood wasn't fit to keep a dog, never mind raise a small boy. "He must have wanted you to know about your past, Ricky." She cast an eye over the dozens of pictures laid out on the dining room table. Many showed Ricky as a child. One in particular caught her eye. It had been taken in someone's sitting room. It must have been Christmas because there was a decorated tree in the corner of the room. Sean had hold of Ricky's hand and was holding another small child in his arms. There was a young woman sitting in a chair to the side. "Are these family too?" she asked Ricky.

"No idea. Looks like the flat we had on the Hobfield when I was growing up, but I hardly remember it. That was before Sean made any real money."

Ruth stared at the photo. It had caught her attention because the young woman looked like Josie Wilkins. If that was the case, then the child Sean was holding could be Jessica. "Can I borrow this?" she asked Ricky. It might be possible to get the photo blown up and see more detail.

"Take what you want. None of it is any use to me. Except those," he nodded to a pile of old documents. "Deeds to the houses Sean owned. Seems my brother was a canny old sod. He had quite a property portfolio. He owned nine houses in Leesworth, all paid for and all currently rented out."

"And you had no idea?"

Ricky ran a hand over his head. "He kept me well in the dark." He looked at Ruth. "It's all legit, so no harm in telling you, there's money I never knew about too. At least the bastard had the sense to put the account in both our names. Means I can get my hands on it, no bother. Now that my brother's gone, it looks like I'm rich."

"I'm pleased for you, Ricky." Ruth smiled. It was just a pity he had no one to share it with. This made her remember the reason for their visit. "You were seeing Flora Appleton, I've been told. Were you close?"

"Not really. She was a bit full-on for my liking. Sean had me working all hours too, so it was difficult. Flora wanted me to take her places, and I wasn't always free. She'd get angry, start mouthing off. In the end I had to finish it. It made life with Sean simpler anyway."

"A shame though, having to ditch your girlfriend because of the job. Couldn't you make Sean see sense?"

"To be honest, I wasn't that bothered. Flora could be a pain sometimes."

"Did you and Sean fight much?" Rocco asked.

"Not at all." Ricky said this without much conviction. "He had a temper on him, but it usually came to nowt. He'd rant and rave a bit, have a couple of drinks and sleep it off."

Rocco nodded at the bruise. "That's a nasty bruise on your cheek. Sean give you that?"

"No! I bumped into a door."

Ruth gave him a sympathetic look. Loyal even after he was gone. She wondered how many times Sean had given the lad a beating. When you got right down to it, Ricky was no better off than all the rest. He suffered from Sean's temper like the others did.

"Handy with his fists and kept you short. Some big brother Sean was. That must have got you down, Ricky?"

Ricky looked at the floor. "Sean was okay," he mumbled. "You don't know owt about him, or our lives."

"You finished with Flora before the festival you'd booked for the pair of you?" Rocco asked.

He nodded. "Cost a bloody bomb too, that did. Something else I could barely afford. I told her Friday morning I couldn't make it. Trouble was, Flora wasn't having any. She kept on at me to go with her. She never stopped texting me all day. In the end, I had to turn off my phone and keep out of her way."

"Did you see Flora that Friday?" said Rocco.

"Not after the morning. I told her I wasn't going to the festival. I was working for the rest of the day, then like I said, I went into hiding."

Rocco looked at him. "Where did you go, Ricky?"

"I went down Manchester, to a restaurant a mate works in. I had something to eat, then sat at the bar for most of the night." He scribbled down a name and address. "He'll vouch for me."

"Did you see or hear from Flora after Friday?"

Ricky shook his head.

Ruth and Rocco turned to leave. At the door, Ruth stopped and looked back at him. "You're a landlord now," she smiled. "A word of advice, don't get heavy with the tenants. You don't want a reputation like your brother's."

His reply surprised them both. "I'm getting shot of the lot of them. This house too. I'm planning on moving away, make a fresh start."

They made their way back to the car. "Speaking of houses, has Nigel found out who owned the one on Beardsell Terrace yet?" Rocco asked.

"I'll ask him when we get back. I can't think what's taking him so long. It should be a simple enough job."

Ruth put the picture carefully in her bag. "The photo is interesting. It could point to a link between Sean Hopwood and Josie Wilkins that we didn't know about."

Chapter 23

"The stab wound is deep," Natasha Barrington said.

Calladine watched Natasha take a ruler to the wound in Sean Hopwood's back.

"It seems to come from below. I'll know more when I open him up."

Nigel Hallam coughed and turned his head away. "Gruesome, isn't it, sir?"

Calladine ignored him. "Might mean the killer was smaller than Hopwood. He was a tall bloke."

Natasha looked up from the body. "Knifed in the back, as I suspected. The blade was long and it pierced the lung. Not content with that, with the knife still deep inside, the killer dragged it horizontally through the chest. It tore into the aorta and the pulmonary artery. He'd have bled out in seconds."

Calladine was thoughtful. "It suggests that whoever killed Hopwood really hated the man. The wound alone was enough to kill him, wasn't it? Someone wanted to make absolutely sure, so they shoved him off the deck for good measure."

Natasha Barrington nodded. "He'd have been dead before he hit the ground. He has multiple broken bones. The X-rays will tell me more. It'll be in the report." She continued to examine the wound in Hopwood's chest. "There is something a little odd here. The wound has a serrated edge on one side. But what's even more interesting, there are traces of what appears to be bread embedded in the flesh. I'll make sure a swab goes off to forensics as soon as."

Calladine was puzzled. "Bread? That's a weird one. How come?"

"Think about it," Nigel interrupted. "It was early, breakfast time. It looks like your victim was attacked with a bread knife that had just been used to cut up a loaf. Perhaps our killer was about to make some toast. There must have been force behind it because it went in deep."

Flora's wounds were consistent with the use of a steak knife. So were the killings linked, or had the killer simply used a different weapon?

Calladine looked at him. "You're saying a spur of the moment thing? Hopwood makes a call, gets a bit rough. The killer's fixing breakfast, speaks to him, knife in hand. Hopwood says the wrong thing and bang! He gets it."

Nigel took up the thread. "He was stabbed in the back, remember. So the killer took a moment, waited until Hopwood had turned round before striking."

"His heart was in a bad way." Natasha looked up at them, holding the organ cupped in her hands. "Heart failure. See how enlarged it is. Without careful monitoring and medication, I'd say his days were numbered anyway."

Nigel shrugged. "Didn't stop him terrorising folk though, did it, sir?"

* * *

The team were assembled in the incident room. Calladine stood by the board, holding a report. "We've had some of the forensics back from the Flora Appleton case.

Nothing useful under her fingernails, which is a shame. But she had clouted someone with enough force to bruise her knuckles. Any ideas?"

"Kyle Logan has a black eye," Ruth said.

"Bernie Logan was beaten up. Who knows what bruises he already had before that happened," Hallam added.

"Anyone else?"

Rocco folded his arms. "Ricky Hopwood is sporting a bruised cheek. He swears he bumped into something. When I suggested that Sean might have lamped him one, he denied it."

Ruth added, "Sean was a bully. I'm sure he did lash out at his brother, but Ricky is embarrassed about it. Ricky isn't like Sean, he has a sensitive side. I bet he felt Sean's fist many times, but he won't admit it. It's his way of protecting his brother. Apart from which, he has given us an alibi for Friday night."

Calladine nodded. "Check that out as soon as. By the way, Flora's leather jacket had traces of heroin in one of the pockets."

"The girl was on drugs?" Ruth looked surprised.

"Or she could have been dealing," Rocco suggested. "A run-in with a rival dealer. Could that be the reason why she was killed?"

"The more we delve into this case, the more mysteries we uncover. I want those kids spoken to again. Ask them about the drugs. Isla Prentice might talk to us. She isn't one of the gang. Plus, we still don't have a proper reason why she left the scene when they found the body." Calladine looked round at them. "Any suspects for the Hopwood killing?"

"Bernie Logan is the obvious one," Rocco said.

"Not Dolly, despite what she told me," said Ruth. "I don't think she has it in her. Anyway, she's grieving for Flora. We now know that a number of people from the Hobfield, including Dolly, met on Tuesday morning to discuss getting rid of Hopwood. That means we have to consider them."

Calladine looked at her. "They all had their problems with Hopwood. Talking is one thing, but like you said, can you really see the likes of Dolly or Frank Chadwick killing anyone?"

Ruth pursed her lips. "There were others, including the Logans."

"Speak to them all, Rocco. Get cast-iron alibis for where they were after that meeting."

Ruth looked at her boss. "I'd like to speak to the Chadwicks myself. What have you done with Dolly?"

"I sent her home," he replied. "She's hardly going to do a runner, is she?"

"Logan's alibi is his son, and Kyle's is his dad. But thanks to Dolly we now know that Bernie Logan was at the meeting, plotting to kill Hopwood. Perhaps that's exactly what he did," Ruth suggested. "He is the only one with form, and he has felt Hopwood's fist of late."

"Ricky?" Nigel suggested, and looked at Rocco.

Ruth shook her head. "We went round that morning. Ricky was just out of bed, fresh from the shower in fact. Anyway, why would he kill his brother? He relied on him for everything. We spoke to him earlier, and the lad is lost. Say's he is moving away, selling everything, including their house, and leaving Leesworth far behind."

Calladine looked round at the team. "Anyone else?"

Ruth sighed. "The more we look, the longer the list becomes. Hopwood hurt people. Take Annie Chadwick, for example. I have been told that when the Chadwicks said they couldn't pay, Hopwood deliberately burnt Annie's hand. I've seen it, it's a nasty wound. We don't know how many more folk there are out there that Hopwood hurt."

"So why didn't the Chadwicks speak out?" Calladine couldn't understand why these people put up with so much, why they kept quiet.

"They were frightened, like most of the people Hopwood dealt with. I intend to talk to them both as soon as."

"Hopwood was killed with what appears to be a bread knife," said Calladine. "Tests are being done, but they've found something that looks like breadcrumbs in the wound. That suggests someone in that block. Breakfast is on the go, Hopwood comes calling, says the wrong thing and the killer loses it."

"That takes us back to Bernie Logan," Rocco said.

"Nigel, have you found out who lived at the house on Beardsell Terrace yet?" Calladine couldn't understand the reason for the delay. Surely it was a simple enough task?

"No. Sorry, sir. It would seem that the house was rented out, and the list of tenants only goes back five years. Prior to that a letting agency dealt with it, but they've since gone out of business."

Calladine sighed with frustration. "Get onto the Land Registry. They will tell you who the actual owner was."

"I did ask that, sir. However, they say there is a missing conveyancing document. They are looking, but don't hold out much hope."

"Get onto them again. Tell them this is a murder enquiry. I want that information on my desk by the end of the day." Calladine turned to the others. "First, we speak to those kids again. Did they know anything about the drugs Flora was carrying? Was she a dealer or a user?"

"If she dealt a little, that could be the reason why they held back," Ruth said.

"Rocco and Nigel, go and round them up. Ruth and I will have another word with Isla Prentice."

Chapter 24

"What haven't those kids told us about Friday night, Ruth? We're missing several pieces of this jigsaw. How and why they met up. When and where they bumped into Kyle, and why Isla disappeared before the police arrived. What was she scared of?"

Calladine and Ruth were waiting in the car outside the Prentice house.

Ruth shrugged. "That could be down to the drugs. If Flora did do a bit of dealing, then Isla and the others would know. Perhaps they were hoping to buy from her. They're hardly going to tell us that, are they?"

"Whoever killed Flora was a novice. The fighting, multiple stab wounds and stuffing her in the boot of the car like that, it all smacks of panic, of not having thought things through."

Ruth nodded. "Just like with Hopwood. Stabbed and lobbed over the deck. But unlike Flora's case, his body was left for anyone to find. Whoever killed him wasn't shy about folk finding out."

"Definitely two different killers," said Calladine.

Ruth smiled. "Thought that from the start."

He gave Ruth the news. "Nigel Hallam is leaving us. Birch told me. He's finding us heavy going, can't settle. What do you think?"

"The sensible part of me says he hasn't given it long enough. But he isn't fitting in. He's the odd one out, and I don't know why."

"We're getting someone else any time now. Some go-getting female graduate with too much ambition."

Ruth grinned. "That'll please Birch. Got a name?"

"No. We'll find out soon enough, I suppose."

* * *

Isla's mum seemed surprised to see them again. She scowled. "I thought Isla told you everything the other day. I don't know what more she can say. We're trying to forget the whole sorry incident."

Calladine smiled at her. "Just a few things to clear up. We won't keep you long."

She grudgingly invited them in, and called up the stairs to Isla.

Isla's tone was sullen. "What now?" She obviously had her guard up. She sat as far away from them as she could, and kept checking her phone.

"You going out, Isla?" Ruth asked.

Isla shrugged. "Waiting for a text. Might meet the lads down the park."

"Would that be Kyle and the others?"

Isla nodded.

Joan Prentice had gone into the kitchen. Ruth used the opportunity to ask the trickier questions Isla might not want her mother to hear.

"Did Flora sell drugs?" she asked quietly.

"No!" Isla's face turned red. "What makes you think that?"

"Okay, not sell, but did she use drugs, buy stuff off the lads maybe?"

Isla stared at the phone in her hands. Eventually she said, "I'm not sure. She got into trouble once, along with Kyle. We all did. Kyle had some blow and we got stopped by a copper on the estate. He dragged us all down the station. We got let off though, and it had nothing to do with me."

"I asked about Flora because we found traces in her pocket." Ruth said.

Isla shrugged. "She might have got something from Kyle. He knows people who sell all sorts. Sometimes he has a little to share around."

"Why did you all meet up last Friday night?" Calladine asked her.

"We just did. We meet all the time. We hang out on the High Street, near the burger bar. But Friday, Dean wanted to go for a ride."

"So there was you, Dean, Jack and Kyle?" Ruth counted them on her fingers.

"We met Kyle later, near the pub where he works. We waited till he'd finished his shift."

Calladine looked at her. "The car was parked up near there too."

"Look, we didn't do any harm. The boys wanted to take the car, go for a ride. They said Marshal wouldn't mind."

Isla kept looking round. She lowered her voice almost to a whisper. "Look, you won't tell my mum about the drugs, will you? I never took anything, not even when Flora offered. But mum would go off on one if she thought I was with anyone who was into drugs."

Ignoring this, Ruth said, "Tell us about the car. Why didn't you take it in the end? Did something put you off?"

Isla grimaced. "The thing stank. There was no way I was even going to sit in it. Besides, Kyle wasn't up for it. He told the lads Marshal had said to get rid. I think he would have too, if we hadn't found Flora."

"What do you mean, get rid?" Calladine asked her.

"Kyle was going to take it up onto the moors and set it alight. He had a can of petrol with him."

Calladine frowned. "How was Kyle? Was he bothered when the lads wanted to take it?"

"He shouted at Dean. Told him to get lost. Said we'd be better off leaving the thing alone. He said he'd get us some beer instead."

"So Kyle wanted you all to leave? To let him get on with destroying the car?" Calladine sat forward.

Isla nodded.

"Why did you leave before the police arrived, Isla?" Ruth asked.

"I got frightened. When we found Flora, Kyle went ballistic. Said we should have left things alone, said we'd interfered, made things worse. He blamed me. He said it was down to me that Dean and Jack had wanted the car. They wanted to show off, impress me. When I saw Flora, I panicked. Kyle got angry. He was shouting and swearing." Isla looked straight at them now, tears running down her young face. "I think it was him that killed her. Nothing else makes sense. I think it was Kyle who put her in that boot."

* * *

"The big question is why Kyle wanted to torch that car. Just gets better and better, doesn't it?" Ruth shook her head.

"We'll be sure to ask him when we get back, Ruth." Calladine rang the station and spoke to Joyce, telling her to make sure that Kyle Logan was held until he returned.

"Of course, he could have been paid to do it," Ruth suggested.

"Then again, Kyle could have known what was in the boot because he put her there, like Isla said."

"You think it was him?" asked Ruth.

"I'm not sure. I'm struggling to find a motive. I can't think of anyone who would hate Flora Appleton enough to want her dead. Kyle was supposed to be her friend. They all went around together."

"Drugs? A mistake?" Ruth looked at him.

"It was a frenzied attack. Whoever killed her was in a right rage. He meant it. That knife was no mistake, Ruth."

They were sitting in the car outside the Prentice house. Calladine was thinking over what Isla had just told them. "Let's see if Ken Marshal is back yet. You never know, he might have something useful to throw into the pot."

They drove the few hundred metres to the block Marshal lived in. His flat was on the second floor, and from the deck he had a clear view of the Pheasant. It was a sunny day. People were standing outside the pub, smoking. Leaning against the wall.

Ruth grinned. "If they put tables and chairs out, someone would nick 'em."

"That's him." Calladine nodded. "The bloke third along, with the donkey jacket on, that's Marshal."

They locked the car and went over. Marshal eyed them warily. As they drew nearer, he put the remainder of his pint on the window sill and started to run.

Calladine shouted after him, "I wouldn't, Marshal! You'd be under lock and key by teatime."

Marshal stopped in his tracks, turned and scowled at them. "None of it has owt do wi' me. I'd no idea what them kids were doing wi' car. I hadn't been near it in weeks."

"All we want is a quick chat, clear up a few things," Calladine told him.

They walked him back to their vehicle. Ruth sat in the driver's seat, while Calladine got in the back with Marshal.

"Rumour has it you wanted rid. Why was that?"

"Because the thing was a heap. Scrapyard wanted money off me to take it away. I couldn't sell it. Thing was an eyesore. Council had been on at me to do something."

"So Kyle comes to your rescue?"

"So what? He's not a bad lad. He knew the score."

"What do you mean, knew the score?" asked Ruth.

"He asked me if I wanted rid. Said if I slipped him a tenner, he'd see to it."

Ruth smiled. "Just like that. Who came up with the idea first? You or Kyle?"

"Like I say, he did. Reckoned he'd take it somewhere and set it alight. No skin off my nose. You lot come knocking, I'd just say it'd been stolen."

Calladine turned to him. "You haven't forgotten that a girl's body was found in the boot?"

"Don't know anything about that, copper. I'm telling you everything. I'm not holding back. I had nowt to do wi' that girl's death. I'd no idea she were even in there."

"When did you last use the car?" asked Calladine.

"I haven't been near in ages. Bloody thing hasn't gone for weeks. It's got no tax nor nothing. The minute I put it on th' road, I'd get done. That's why I stuck it over there."

"Okay, that'll do for now. But don't do another disappearing act. We might need to speak to you again."

Marshal got out and slammed the car door behind him.

"Do you believe him?" Calladine asked Ruth.

"He was perfectly honest about getting rid of the thing. He admitted he was happy for Kyle to torch it."

"The question is, why would Kyle want to do that?"

Chapter 25

"I want to speak to those three lads one at a time," Calladine told the duty sergeant. "I'll start with Kyle Logan. Stick him in an interview room and I'll be along in a minute. And arrange for DNA samples and fingerprints to be taken from all of them."

Calladine went to the incident room to ring the Duggan. It was mid-afternoon, but Julian had already left for the day. He spoke to Roxy Atkins. "Have you found any further forensic evidence in the Flora Appleton case?"

"There are one or two things," Roxy confirmed. "There was a smudged print on the earring. Finally we got a partial. Not Flora's, and no match on the database I'm afraid. However, Mrs Appleton recognised the earring, and she reckons the hair is Flora's. We went back and had another look at the spot where the killing took place. It has rained very heavily so I wasn't hopeful. But — we found minute traces of blood on some blades of grass. Of course, it could belong to Flora, but if we're very lucky it'll be the killer's. We know that Flora put up a fight. It's being processed as we speak. I'll let you know if it throws up anything."

"Speed would be appreciated. We're struggling to sort this one," Calladine told her. "There's plenty who'd do for Hopwood, but Flora is another matter. No one that we've looked at so far has a motive. I'm about to interview the three lads who found her. Their stories don't match up. I'll send you their DNA samples and fingerprints, for elimination if nothing else."

"It has priority, Tom," Roxy promised him.

"What with all the excitement, I forgot to show you this." Ruth pulled the photo out of her pocket. "Who do you reckon that is?"

Calladine looked at the old snap carefully. "That could be Hopwood," he decided.

"Yes, it is, and the little lad whose hand he's holding is Ricky. The woman sat in the chair? What do you think?"

Calladine saw the likeness straight away. He'd seen a lot of Josie Wilkins at one time. "You think this is Josie? You could be right. It's the longer hair. She had it like that back then, I remember. Sometimes she used to scrape it back into a ponytail." He paused. "That would mean that the child in Hopwood's arms is Jessica."

"Ricky can't remember the occasion, but it has to be Christmas. Look at the tree."

"I'd no idea they were that friendly. I wonder if it was Tracy who took this. I'll make a copy, but can we keep hold of the original?"

"Ricky has hundreds of photos, all left to him by Sean. He doesn't know who the people are in most of them. So, yes, he'll be fine with it."

"We'll speak to Kyle first. Then I think I might go and have a word with Tracy Wilkins."

* * *

"Tell me about Marshal's car, Kyle," Calladine began. "Start with whose idea it was to get rid of it."

"It were his. Marshal wanted rid. When he told me, I offered to help." Kyle shrugged as if this was obvious.

"He reckons it was your idea. He reckons you were keen to see the car gone."

"It was just a random conversation in the bar one night. He said the thing was causing problems, I said get rid, and he asked me to help."

"Are you sure?"

Kyle nodded. "Yeah, that's how it happened. Why the interest anyway?"

Ruth rolled her eyes. "I'm surprised you even ask. Because Flora was found dead in the boot. Why do you think? You wanting to lose the car does suggest that you knew that, Kyle."

"Now you're twisting things! I was as shocked as the others when we found Flora."

"When did you last see her alive?" Calladine asked.

"That Friday, the day she went missing. She came in the Pheasant, looking for Ricky."

"Are you sure?" asked Calladine. Wallace had maintained he hadn't seen her.

"Yeah, she was in just before eight. Some bloke bought her a drink. She stood at the bar chatting to him."

"What bloke?"

Kyle shrugged. "No idea. Never seen him before."

"Was Wallace in that night?" Calladine asked.

"I can't run the place on my own. Course he was there."

"Would he know who this man was?"

Kyle shrugged again.

"You gave your dad an alibi. You said he was in the flat when Hopwood was killed. He wasn't though, was he, Kyle?"

Calladine watched Kyle wrestle with this. "He didn't do it," he said at last. "He can be a sod at times, but he wouldn't kill anyone, not even Hopwood."

"Do you know where he was that morning?"

Kyle shook his head. "Can I go now? I've got work."

Calladine leaned forward and looked into his face. “You lie about your dad. You’re cagey about Marshal’s car. You can see how this looks, can’t you, Kyle? Until I get credible answers, something I can believe, you’ll be staying here with us. Okay, that’ll do for now.”

Chapter 26

"Do you reckon Kyle's our man?" Ruth said.

"I don't know, Ruth. I'm struggling to come up with a motive. No one we've spoken to so far had a beef with Flora. Granted, she wasn't universally liked. According to her mother, she could be a feisty madam at times. But did she upset someone enough for them to kill her?" Calladine replied.

"She upset someone. A frenzied attack, remember."

Rocco and Nigel had interviewed Dean and Jack. They too had made no progress. Neither of those two had a reason to kill Flora either.

"Where to now?" asked Nigel.

"Beardsell Terrace," Calladine reminded him. "If you plan to go home tonight, I'd find that information."

The office phone rang. "There is a woman downstairs asking for you, sir," said Joyce.

"Name?"

Joyce shook her head. "She is expected apparently."

Ruth smiled. "The new DC? Come for a nosey round, no doubt."

Calladine hadn't given the new detective much thought. He hadn't even got round to speaking to Nigel Hallam about him leaving yet. Hopefully he would stay with them a bit longer. He wasn't in the mood for all that. There was too much going on to waste time showing a new DC the ropes.

"Inspector Calladine!" The young woman stuck out her hand. "It's been a while."

Calladine blinked. "Alice? It is Alice Bolshaw, isn't it?"

A grin spread across her face and she nodded. "Fresh from two years spent on the beat in Sheffield. I couldn't wait for my transfer to CID to come through, and I was lucky enough to get the job with you."

Calladine and the team had met Alice Bolshaw on a previous case. Alice was still at university then. She'd joined them briefly on work experience, and had been a great help in solving the case. Calladine couldn't get over how she'd changed. The Alice of old had been a prim, old-fashioned-looking girl in pleated skirts, buttoned up blouses and sensible shoes. There had never been a scrap of make-up on her face, and her long hair was always tied up in a bun. The Alice that greeted him now was another person entirely. Loose, fair hair hung down her back. Her legs were encased in skinny jeans, ripped at the knees, and topped with a low cut T-shirt. She looked utterly different.

She laughed. "A hefty dose of real life changes people. God knows what I was thinking back then. You must have thought I was a right nerd."

"We all thought you were a great help, as it happens. You had things worked out way before we did."

She gave him another grin. "I still make lists. But I think I'll fit in a bit better now. Are the others still here?"

"Ruth and Rocco are, yes. Do you know about what happened to Imogen?"

"Yes, I'm so sorry. I liked her. She was a role model for me. I wanted to be like her."

"Come upstairs and we'll surprise the others. I'm sure they'll be pleased to see you."

And they were, particularly Rocco. He turned to the others. "I've a confession to make. We've been seeing each other."

Ruth smiled. "So Alice is your little secret! You could have said."

"No, I couldn't. You'd have told everyone. Alice didn't want that, not before she got here anyway."

Calladine wasn't sure what he thought. He was still getting over the shock of how Alice looked. Now it turned out that she and Rocco were an item. That would take some getting used to. They'd never had a romance within the team before. It could be tricky.

"Now you're here, familiarise yourself with the cases we're working on. We've two murders and a cold case. It will be interesting to have a fresh pair of eyes look at them. I'm calling it a day. I will call in and speak to Tracy Wilkins on my way home. See you all tomorrow."

* * *

Tracy lived on the floor above her sister. Calladine had brought the photo with him. He was curious to see what she made of it. He didn't want Josie involved at this point. If something untoward had happened all those years ago, he didn't want Josie unnecessarily upset.

It was way past seven when Calladine knocked on Tracy's door. She didn't look too pleased to see him.

"What now?"

Calladine smiled at her. "I'd like you to help me with something. Can I come in?"

She stood aside and followed him into the sitting room. "Josie's coming for tea, so make it snappy," she said.

He handed her the photo.

Tracy Wilkins studied it for a good few seconds, and then handed it back. "So? What's this supposed to mean?"

"It means that Josie knew Sean Hopwood well enough back then to have him and Ricky around at Christmas. I'd like to know about that relationship, and why no one ever mentioned it."

"It wasn't important, that's why. One photo. It means nothing."

"Did you take it?"

Her shoulders drooped. "Yes."

"So tell me, what was going on?"

"Nothing. We were neighbours, that's all. Hopwood had a young brother to look after, Josie had Jess. It was Christmas, and we thought it would be nice for the kids to play together."

Calladine shook his head. "Josie hated Hopwood. He was constantly at her for money."

"Not then, he wasn't. He hadn't started up the loan business in those days. That came later. He wasn't up to much, but he was okay. He'd brought Ricky up from an early age, and he was a neighbour. We didn't have much, and he'd bought presents for Jess. Josie invited him and Ricky to spend the day with us."

"Why didn't you or Josie ever say you'd been pally with Hopwood at one time?"

"Because it wasn't important. As time passed, we wanted people forgetting that we'd had anything to do with Hopwood. We didn't want folk round here thinking bad of us. And they would have," she said bitterly. "Josie wouldn't have stood a chance."

"You should have said something when Jessica disappeared. You had no right holding back information like that."

"Stuff you! What difference did it make? None! Hopwood lived on the same deck. You must have spoken to him along with all the others."

"What really happened, Tracy?"

She turned away from him. “You know what happened. Josie was at the park and someone took Jess from the pushchair.”

Calladine stared at her back, willing her to turn round. “I’ve looked at the case files again. I don’t think it was as simple as you make out.”

Chapter 27

Thursday

The following morning, Ruth and Calladine were sitting in the incident room. "Alice said something interesting last night," began Ruth. "It was about the Jessica Wilkins case. She pointed out that someone had taken great care with Jessica's ashes. The jar is valuable, it's no trinket. And the way the jar was placed in the fireplace. Whoever put it there didn't want it falling over or being dislodged accidently. Alice suggested a close relative, someone who loved the child."

Calladine nodded. "Alice is going to be good. Although we had already noticed that. Anything else, anything on the Flora case?"

"Only what we'd been thinking. Who had she upset? Her family? Her boyfriend, Ricky?"

"Her only family is her mother, and I doubt she killed her. But Ricky? What do you think?"

"I don't know what I think anymore. I plan to have a talk with the Chadwicks this morning. Once I've got that done and dusted I'll speak to Roly, that homeless bloke. We could tackle Ricky together perhaps. After lunch?"

Calladine nodded. "Do we know who owned Beardsell Terrace yet?"

"Nigel left a note on your desk. Apparently he won't be in today. He's off for a visit to his new station."

Calladine went to his office. Nigel had left him a list of everyone who had rented the property during the last twenty years. No one stood out. There were no familiar names, no one linked to the case. The owner for the five years after Jessica disappeared was a man called Bob Seward, a property developer from Halifax. He'd had the house done up, then rented it out. Calladine would get Rocco to ring him.

That house had to be significant in some way. Otherwise why put her there, and take so much trouble over it?

He couldn't get over the fact that Josie and Hopwood had been friends. It didn't sit right. Hopwood might have gotten worse over the years but even in his younger days, he'd not been someone you'd want as a friend. He would have to speak to Josie. Tracy could like it or lump it. In the meantime he'd see if forensics could help. He rang Roxy Atkins.

"Do you have any DNA results on the items from Beardsell Terrace?" he asked her.

"We're dealing with bone, Tom, bone that has been burned, so it's way too soon, if ever. What are you thinking?"

"I want it compared with Sean Hopwood's DNA."

"Interesting idea. Is this a hunch, or do you have something?" she asked.

"A hunch that's niggling me. Never mind. I'll think of something else."

Her next words came as a surprise. "No need. We still have the child's DNA on the database from seventeen years ago. That is what you're thinking, isn't it? Checking Jessica's with Hopwood's?"

"Will you do that for me? I don't know how it will help, but it's worth a shot."

Calladine returned to the incident room. Ruth had left and taken Rocco with her. Nigel had done his disappearing act.

"Joyce, would you get onto the Land Registry again? This list Nigel did earlier is all very well but it tells us nothing. There has to be a reason why the ashes were put in that particular house."

* * *

"She's changed a lot, your Alice," Ruth said.

"Nothing to do with me, Ruth. When we met again on that course, I didn't recognise her straight off. She knew me though." Rocco grinned. "She's been through a lot. Helped on some tough cases during her time at Sheffield. Alice should be okay. She's not afraid of getting stuck in."

"You don't have to convince me. I liked her then, and I like her now. She's bright. It's just what the team needs, fresh blood."

"That was supposed to be Nigel," he replied.

Ruth shrugged. "Hasn't worked, has it? Not worth wasting time trying to analyse why, it was just one of those things."

Rocco looked at her. "You don't really suspect Frank Chadwick, do you? I read the notes in the file. He's seventy-five. Would he even be capable of taking on a man like Hopwood?"

Ruth bit her bottom lip. She really wanted to believe that Frank was innocent, but there was a nagging doubt at the back of her mind. "I don't know. But given what Dolly told me, we have to speak to him. Annie's injury gives him a motive."

"Surely there has to be someone else. This whole estate hated Hopwood."

"It looks like it was done on the spur of the moment, Rocco. If it was premeditated, then I'd agree with you. Just think. Hopwood knocks at the door. It's early, Frank and Annie are getting breakfast. Hopwood is his usual obnoxious self, says or does something that gets to Frank and he loses it. Fired up and angry, I think Frank would be capable."

They left the car outside the community centre, where there were plenty of people around. The Heron House lift was actually working. Things were looking up. That lasted until they arrived at Frank Chadwick's flat. Two paramedics were carrying him out.

Ruth ran forward and put her arm around Annie. "What's happened?"

"It's his chest, love. It's being playing him up for days. But he were taken really badly this morning. They're taking him to the infirmary." Annie began to sob.

"Frank has COPD," Ruth told Rocco.

"Comes from working in th' cotton mill when he were younger," Annie added.

The paramedics had an oxygen mask clamped to Frank's face. There was no chance of talking to him for the time being.

* * *

Ruth turned to Rocco. "Let's go and find Roly."

"What? That down and out?"

"That down and out is a mine of information. And he lives the way he does by choice. He describes himself as a free spirit." Ruth smiled. "He'll be in the community centre. It's cheap breakfast day."

Roly was at a table by the door with an empty plate and a full mug of tea in front of him.

"Go and get us a couple of coffees," Ruth told Rocco.

Roly nodded to an empty chair. "Sit down, lass."

"How long have you been back?" Ruth asked him.

"A couple of weeks. Not hanging around though. Two folk have got themselves killed on here lately. It's not safe."

"We're on it, Roly. You are in no danger."

Roly poured enough sugar into his tea to fill the mug. "No, you're not! You're looking in t' wrong place."

"What d'you mean?"

"Take that lass they found in Marshal's car. Leading them lads a right dance she was. She were arguing with them that night. I heard them going at it by the Pheasant."

Ruth leaned forward. "On the Friday night, Roly?"

"Yes. Like I said, going at it real bad they were. She came off best though. First she had a go at Logan's lad, then she met up with t'other one. Don't know what she said, but he were fuming. Chased after her, he did.

"Who chased her, Roly?"

"That Hopwood's brother, Ricky. They disappeared round the back of the pub. Screaming and shouting at him, she was."

"Then what happened?"

"That other lad, the one who works in the pub, he took Ricky back there. Ricky looked to be in a bad way. He weren't happy, that's for sure."

"Did Kyle argue with Flora?"

Roly shrugged. "I don't know. There were a lot of noise."

"You're sure it was young Hopwood she was having a go at?"

He nodded.

"What were they arguing about? Did you hear?"

"She had money, I know that. The lass kept flashing it about. But I never saw her part with any."

Chapter 28

Calladine was poring over the Jessica Wilkins file when Ruth burst into his office.

"A witness reckons that Flora was near the Pheasant on that Friday night. She was arguing with Ricky Hopwood — at least, until Kyle Logan interfered."

"What witness? We've spoken to every single person on that damned estate."

"Roly, the homeless bloke I told you about."

"You believe him?" Calladine asked.

"He has no reason to lie. He's told me stuff before, and it's always been spot on."

Calladine pushed the Wilkins file to one side. Ricky Hopwood? That didn't make much sense. He had been seeing Flora. Even though he didn't want to go to the festival with her, they hadn't fallen out. Calladine was struggling to find a reason for it. But it did mean that Ricky's alibi was shot. So why lie?

But Kyle Logan was another matter. He had wanted to torch Marshal's car. Did he know that Flora's body was in the boot?

"So Wallace was lying. Ricky Hopwood was in or around the pub that night. We'll have to have another word with them both." What reason would Wallace have for watching Ricky's back? Calladine wondered. "Okay, we'll bring Kyle in first. When we've questioned him, we'll decide what to do about Ricky."

"What about Bernie?" asked Ruth.

"We'll bring them both in. I'll send uniform to fetch them."

"I still haven't spoken to the Chadwicks," Ruth told him. "Frank was being taken to hospital when we turned up. His chest is bad again."

"Rocco has interviews sorted with the others. The nurse, John Barnett, went straight to work from the cricket club in a taxi. The other two are coming in later. That leaves us with Bernie Logan. He has no alibi either," Calladine told her.

He went out to the incident room and handed Rocco an address and phone number. "It's a restaurant in Manchester. Ricky Hopwood reckons he was there all last Friday night. I don't think he was, but check it out anyway, will you?"

Calladine's mobile rang. It was Julian from the Duggan.

"Roxy tells me you were looking for DNA from the child to compare with that of Sean Hopwood," he said.

"Yes, Julian. Do you have anything?"

"You were right to be curious. I ran the child's DNA through the database again. Sean Hopwood was her father."

Calladine shoved a fist into the palm of his other hand. That was it! He'd known there was something. All he had to do now was find out why no one had said anything. Why keep it so secret? "Thanks, Julian. I don't know where this little snippet will get us, but it could be significant."

"What are you up to?" Ruth appeared beside him.

"That photo you gave me, the one of the Hopwoods and Josie. It had me curious about the relationship."

She looked at him. "What do you mean?"

"Josie and her sister are the only people who know who Jessica's father was. I got to thinking — and Julian has just confirmed my suspicions — Sean Hopwood was Jessica's father." He was pleased with himself.

"Interesting, but where does that get us?"

"I don't know, but I have this hunch that it is significant. And why haven't Josie or Tracy said anything about the affair?"

Calladine was thinking. Only the team and the people at the Duggan knew that Jessica had been shot. Was it possible that it had gotten out somehow? Calladine knew what the Hobfield jungle drums were like. If the information had leaked, would that give Josie or Tracy a motive for killing Hopwood?

"I'd like to know why they never told us at the time. As I recall, I don't even remember Hopwood being particularly interested in Jessica's disappearance."

"Perhaps he didn't know he was the dad," Ruth suggested.

"I think he did. Hence the attempt at a family Christmas."

Calladine now felt sure that both Josie and Tracy were hiding something important. The more they dug, the more questions arose. Sooner or later, he was going to have to tackle Josie.

* * *

The Logans were brought in separately. Bernie had kicked off the minute the police knocked on the door. He was still shouting when they dragged him into the interview room.

One of the uniformed officers passed Calladine in the corridor. "Got your brave head on?" he said. "You'll need it. That's one angry man."

Calladine and Rocco settled into their seats facing Logan. "Why the performance? All we want is a quiet chat," said Calladine.

"Every time something happens, you beat a path to my door. Well, I'm sick of it! Me and Kyle, we've done nowt."

"Not entirely true. You met with some others at the cricket club on Tuesday morning. What was that all about?"

Logan's candid reply came as a surprise. "Getting rid of Hopwood," he said simply. "We were all bloody sick of him and his violence. Everyone there had suffered. We all wanted rid, not just me."

"Did one of you kill him?"

"How the hell should I know? But it wasn't me, if that's what this is all about. I went home. Kyle was in bed. But make no mistake, copper. If the opportunity had presented itself, I would have been straight in there."

"Can anyone vouch for you?"

"No." Logan shifted on the chair. "Hang on, there is someone. I walked back to the flats with her from the community centre — you know, her that runs the café. She collared me and asked if I'd look at the sink. It keeps blocking up."

"How long did you stay?"

"Half an hour, but then she gave me breakfast. I must have got home just after nine thirty."

Hopwood was dead by then.

"I'm surprised you didn't see the crowd gathering," said Calladine.

"Went in the back way with Angus the postman. He was telling me about the match on Saturday."

"In that case you do have alibis, Bernie. You could have saved yourself all this by telling us the first time around. Or were you protecting Kyle?"

Logan grunted. "Kyle had no beef with Hopwood. Whenever Sean came calling, Kyle were always out. It were me that took the brunt of his temper."

Calladine looked at him. "Are you telling me the truth?"

"I think so. But I've been forgetting things of late. That was a damn good beating Hopwood gave me the other night. I've had a sore head ever since."

"Go and see your doctor, that's my advice. We'll check out what you've told us. If it holds up, then you are in the clear."

"And Kyle?"

"Kyle is here on a different matter."

* * *

Kyle wasn't as mouthy as his father. In fact, he didn't say a word.

Calladine sat down opposite him and began immediately. "I want a blow by blow account of what happened the Friday night Flora was killed."

Kyle shrugged. "Told you. Don't know owt. I was working."

"We know you were, but we have a witness who saw and heard you arguing with Flora outside the Pheasant." Kyle inhaled. He stared up at the ceiling.

"You won't find the answer up there, lad. Tell us what happened."

Kyle sighed. "Flora was looking for Ricky. She said they'd arranged to meet. But I knew Ricky was sick of her. Whatever had been going on between them, he wanted out. Flora was in the pub shouting her head off. Wallace told me to get shut of her."

"What did you do?" asked Calladine.

"I took her outside. I rang Ricky's mobile but got no answer. In the end, Flora got fed up and wandered off. I went back to work."

"Did Ricky turn up?"

"Yes, eventually. He came in the pub and I told him about Flora. He went outside to look for her. And before you ask, I don't know what was going on between them. But I heard Flora mouthing off. I don't know what she said to him, but Ricky was right cut up. He came back into the pub and had a drink. I told him she wasn't worth the trouble."

"Did you see anyone else hanging about?"

"I wasn't looking. The pub was busy. There was a lot of folk milling around."

"Why so secretive then? What are you both trying to hide?"

"It's the whole Flora thing. We start telling you about the row and you lot will assume it was either me or Ricky that killed her."

"It was you who wanted to torch that car. Did you know what was in the boot?"

"No! I was doing Marshal a favour, earning a bit of spare cash."

"Rubbish. You wouldn't go to all that trouble just for a tenner. So come on, Kyle, what was really going on?"

"I've said enough. You need to speak to Ricky. I had nothing to do with killing Flora."

"You didn't want the others going near that car though, did you?"

The silence almost hummed. Calladine watched Kyle Logan wrestle with himself. Would he speak? Was he protecting Ricky? If so, what for? Money. That had to be the answer.

Chapter 29

"We'll keep Kyle for a while longer, but you can let Bernie go home. Suddenly he's got alibis coming out of his ears." Calladine rubbed his head. "Kyle is another matter. Both him and Ricky have a lot more to say."

Ruth looked at him. "Has he landed Ricky in it?"

"Ricky did meet Flora on the night she was killed. Your friend Roly said as much, and Kyle confirmed it. We will have to bring him in."

"Are we sending uniform?"

"No. We'll pick him up ourselves. A casual little chat in the car on the way back here will do no harm. I'm curious to know what Ricky recalls from his early childhood."

"So if Bernie didn't kill Sean Hopwood, who did?"

Calladine shook his head. "I've got no idea. It could be anyone on that damned estate. They all hated the man."

"I'll have a word with the Chadwicks later. How about the others who were at that meeting?"

"Rocco says they are all sound. Alibis check out. So no joy."

Ruth stared accusingly at the incident board. "Are we getting anywhere with this? The more we know, the more there is to find out."

"We'll get there." Calladine spoke with a confidence that he didn't feel. The job was getting harder — or he was getting slower, he wasn't sure which.

They set off for the Hopwood house. "How are you and Jake doing?" Calladine asked.

"Well, we are talking now. Jake is right, it's a great school, and this new job wouldn't do his career any harm. It all boils down to whether or not I could stomach the move."

Ruth was driving, negotiating a busy roundabout.

Her tone had been so matter of fact. "And could you?" Calladine thought his voice sounded funny. It certainly did to him. This wasn't looking good.

"What do you think I should do?" She was looking at the road ahead.

"Please don't ask me that, it's not fair. I want you with me. This job needs us both."

She gave him a quick glance. "Don't be so soft. You don't need me."

"That's where you're wrong. I'd hate it if you moved away. I don't want to work with anyone else."

"Now you sound like a spoilt child! You've got Rocco. He's due a leg up. You'd soon settle."

Calladine couldn't tell if she was being serious. He felt sick. "I wouldn't *settle*, as you put it." He was quiet for a moment or two. "I'd retire, that's what I'd do. Want to be responsible for that?"

Ruth suddenly pulled up at the side of the road. "I've never heard such utter rubbish, Tom Calladine! That's nothing less than emotional blackmail."

"I'm just saying, that's all. I'm getting on now. Early fifties, it's old for a copper. Anyway, I might enjoy retirement."

"You'd like retirement about as much as I'd like living down south! So give up and put your face straight."

"You were joking?" His expression brightened.

Ruth smiled at him. "Sort of. I'm not giving up my job anyway, so relax. I don't know what this teaching job will mean for me and Jake. But I've made my position clear, and he accepts it."

They drove on in silence, Calladine with a grin on his face. He felt like a man who'd just had a narrow escape. For a moment there, the bottom had dropped out of his world.

Ruth nodded towards the car in the driveway. "Here we are. Do we really think he's capable of killing Flora? I know he had Sean for a role model, but Ricky has never struck me as the violent type. This could be a big mistake."

"Let's see what he has to say for himself first."

Inside, the house was very different from their first visit. It looked as if Ricky had emptied every cupboard and drawer in the place. Stuff was strewn all over the floor and every piece of furniture.

Calladine blinked. "Looking for something?"

"I'm selling up," Ricky replied. "Now that Sean is gone, there's nothing to keep me here."

"Ricky, we need to speak to you again. We have a witness who saw you near the Pheasant with Flora on the Friday she was killed."

Ricky Hopwood had been picking things up and dropping them. He stopped, stood up straight and looked at the two detectives. "Whoever it is, they're lying! I told you, I went into Manchester that Friday night. Ask my friend with the restaurant."

"We're having that checked right now," Calladine told him.

Ricky flushed and looked down. "Okay, I might have got the night wrong. Don't blame my friend Josh. He thinks he's doing me a favour. But I didn't harm Flora, I swear. I wouldn't, I liked her."

"So you did see her that night?"

He nodded. "I arranged to meet her. I had no choice. She was being disruptive in the pub and Kyle was scared she'd try to trash the place."

"They could have called the police. She was underage. I thought the plan was to avoid Flora." Calladine was puzzled. "That festival you didn't want to go to? Is that why she was looking for you?"

Ricky sighed. "Things got complicated."

"You will have to come with us, Ricky. We'll talk more down at the station."

"Are you arresting me?"

Calladine could see the confusion on his face. Ricky was in trouble, and for the first time in his life he didn't have Sean to bail him out.

"We need to clear up a few things," Ruth told him kindly.

"Can I have a solicitor?"

Calladine nodded. "If you want one."

"This is him." Ricky handed Adrian Hampson's card to Ruth. "Would you get him for me?"

They drove back to the station in silence. Ricky stared out of the window, his face expressionless. At the station he was put in an interview room until his solicitor arrived. Neither Calladine nor Ruth knew what to expect. Calladine wanted to keep an open mind, but he couldn't forget that Ricky was a Hopwood. Ruth, on the other hand, thought the young man was sound.

"I'll interview him with Rocco," Calladine decided. "That'll leave you free to talk to the Chadwicks."

"Provided Frank is in a fit state. I'll ring the hospital first. Look, Tom, don't be too hard on Ricky."

"It was your friend Roly who gave us the information that put him in the frame. You can hardly blame me. I have no choice but to act on it."

Chapter 30

The ED at Leesdon General confirmed that Frank Chadwick had been treated and sent home. Ruth decided to have that chat with them on her own. Rocco was interviewing Ricky with Calladine. Nigel had finally shown his face, and was reading through the alibis of the people who'd taken part in the meeting to discuss Sean Hopwood.

Ruth wasn't looking forward to this. She knew Frank from the birding group. His wife, Annie, helped to organise the trips. She sighed. It was her job to find the truth. That was what she had to do, and hopefully it would be enough to eliminate the Chadwicks from the enquiry.

Heron House was unusually quiet. No shouting. No shrieking kids tearing along the decks. The killings were finally getting to folk. Ruth knocked on the Chadwicks' front door. Annie poked her head out.

Ruth smiled. "Can I have a word? I know Frank is poorly, so I won't keep you long."

"He's been dreadful. At one point this afternoon I thought he was a goner." Annie led the way inside. "He's in there, love, sat by the fire."

It was a warm day but there was a gas fire roaring away in the sitting room. It was oppressively hot. Frank was sitting practically on top of it, wrapped in a blanket.

"They've given me oxygen," he said. "There's nowt much else they can do."

The tank was behind his chair. "I'm sorry, Frank. What happened to bring this on?"

"Walked too far. Overdid it. You'd think I'd know better, man in my condition."

"What is it you want, love? Is it about the trip?" Annie asked.

Ruth had forgotten all about the birding trip. She doubted she'd be going now. Work was stacking up, and she still had Jake and his new job to deal with.

"I'm here about Sean Hopwood, Annie," she replied.

Annie and her husband exchanged furtive glances.

"I know you went to the meeting with Dolly and the others at the cricket club, Frank. What I need you tell me now is what you did after that."

"Dolly Appleton been blabbing, has she? Can't blame her. She's got enough on her plate as it is." He looked up at Ruth. "I came home, love. Had some breakfast then went up to my allotment."

"Did anyone see you? Did you talk to anyone, Frank?" Same old questions.

He shook his head. "Don't think so. It were early. There was no one about."

"Have you had your hand seen to, Annie?"

"I went down the health centre like you said. The nurse did it for me and the doctor gave me some pills. It'll be right soon."

Ruth jumped. Frank had banged his walking stick against the wall. "It'll never be right, woman!" he shouted. "That bastard hurt you so bad you can hardly use that hand!"

His face crumpled and he started to cry. Annie rushed to his side, and tried to comfort him. Ruth watched, horrified that she'd caused this upset. Frank was gasping for every breath again.

After a while, he patted Annie's arm. "It's no use. I'm going to tell her. They'll find out anyway in time." He kissed his wife's cheek and turned to Ruth.

"I was furious, love. He hurt my Annie real bad. Not content with that, he has the cheek to come round here bothering us again. Threatened to do her other hand. Stood there at the front door, shaking his fist and spouting obscenities. Said it'd be the last time she cooked breakfast or anything else if we didn't pay up."

"You should have rung us straight away," Ruth told him. "We would have stopped Hopwood, Frank. All it would have taken was witnesses willing to speak out."

"We didn't have time to mess about. He had hold of Annie and would have hurt her there and then. I couldn't have that again. I'm not a strong man but I had to stop him. I saw red. I grabbed the bread knife from Annie and put paid to the bugger once and for all."

Ruth closed her eyes. Now she'd have to arrest the poor man, and he was in no state. She needed to speak to Calladine.

* * *

They sent a female uniformed officer to sit with the Chadwicks. Ruth looked at her boss, and her eyes pleaded. "Self-defence? They are elderly. Frank is no match for a man like Hopwood. He did the only thing he could at the time."

Calladine shook his head. "It's not for us to say. Hopwood was stabbed with real force. Frank knew what he was doing. We'll take a statement and go from there. See what the CPS have to say."

"He can't go to prison, Tom. It'd kill him."

"We'll simply have to wait and see. The good news is that we can cross one murder off the list. Now all we have to do is find out who killed Flora."

Chapter 31

Ricky Hopwood sat beside his solicitor in silence. He was debating what to tell the police. Adrian Hampson advised the truth, but if Ricky did that, he knew they would try to pin Flora's murder on him.

He turned to Hampson. "I want out of here. They've kept us waiting around for ages. Surely they can't do that?"

"Calm down. It will be over soon. Do as I say. If I give you the nod, keep your mouth shut."

"I didn't do anything! I'm not Sean. I don't go around hurting people."

"The police wouldn't have brought you in if they didn't have a sound reason for doing so. You would do well to talk to me, Ricky. At least so I know what we are up against."

"They think I had something to do with the murder of Flora Appleton."

"And did you?"

"No!"

"The police are acting on information they've been given."

"They've got it wrong."

"If you are telling the truth, if you had nothing to do with the girl's death, then tell them what happened. Whatever it might look like to you, it is better than spinning a web of lies. The police aren't stupid. They will soon find out that you lied, and it won't go well for you."

* * *

Calladine and Rocco entered the interview room. Calladine smiled. "Sorry to keep you, Ricky. I've got a couple of questions, if you don't mind."

Calladine looked at the two men sitting in front of him. Ricky Hopwood looked pissed off. As for the solicitor, he looked like a man who'd been dragged into something decidedly dodgy, and wanted to be anywhere but here. "A witness has come forward. They have told us you were in and around the Pheasant on the Friday Flora Appleton was killed." Calladine paused, watching the young man's reactions. Ricky looked at the table in front of him.

"Reliable, is he, your witness?" Hampson asked.

"Actually we have more than one," Calladine said. "So come on, Ricky, what really happened that night?"

Ricky kept his eyes on the table. "She'd been hounding me about that bloody festival all day. In the end I agreed to see her at the pub. But when I arrived, Flora wasn't there. Barman told me she'd been talking to Kyle then left. I don't know what she did after that. I had a pint and went home."

Calladine watched him. The words rolled easily from Ricky's lips, but he doubted they were true. "Why didn't you tell us that in the beginning?"

"Sean told me not to. He said you'd blame me for Flora's death. He said once you knew I'd been anywhere near, you wouldn't bother looking at anyone else."

"Your brother was wrong. We're only interested in the truth. Want to start again?"

"No. It's like I just said."

"Kyle tells it differently."

"It's got nothing to do with Kyle."

"He was there, he spoke to Flora. He says you did too, and then you went back into the pub after."

Ricky turned to his solicitor. "Can't you put a stop to this?"

"No, he can't," said Calladine. "You saw Flora that night. You may even have argued with her. This isn't a trap, Ricky. Just tell us what happened."

"I didn't kill her. She was fine when I left."

"But you did see her and you did argue."

"We were always arguing. There was no pleasing Flora sometimes."

"What did you fight about?"

"It wasn't a fight," Ricky insisted. "I didn't hit her or anything."

"Perhaps I should have a word with my client alone," Hampson suggested. "It could benefit everyone."

Calladine nodded. Hampson might well instruct Ricky to come clean and tell them the truth. He certainly hoped so.

* * *

Calladine and Rocco returned to the incident room. Both Kyle and Ricky had admitted to seeing Flora that night. Now he just needed one of them to say what had happened.

"Roxy Atkins has been on. She'd like a word," said Ruth.

Calladine disappeared into his office and closed the door.

"That blood we found on the blades of grass," Roxy began. "It doesn't match the DNA profiles of anyone involved in the case, and there is no match on record."

That surprised Calladine. "Not Kyle Logan or Ricky Hopwood?"

"No," she replied. "And neither of the two other boys who found the body. It also rules out Mark Wallace, landlord of the Pheasant. Given that the murder happened within the vicinity of his pub, I checked the database. He's been in trouble before so his DNA is on record. You're looking for someone you haven't considered yet. That blood was found at the same spot as Flora's body. We know from her hands that Flora fought her attacker."

Calladine heaved a sigh. This wasn't getting any more straightforward. He thanked Roxy.

Another word with Kyle and Ricky was called for. They'd both seen Flora, but who else was there?

Chapter 32

Friday

They'd had to release both Ricky and Kyle. Their stories tallied, and the blood that had been found wasn't theirs. However, Calladine was still sure they both knew more than they'd told him.

It was early, and like most days this week, he was first in the office. He stood staring at the incident board. What were they missing? A stroppy, teenage girl, popular with the boys, Flora had enjoyed more freedom than perhaps her mother should have allowed. Calladine had checked the records. Flora Appleton had rarely been in any trouble. But there had been something. Kyle Logan had been brought in a few times, but had been lucky enough to get off with warnings. On one occasion, Flora had been brought in with him and Isla Prentice too.

Nigel Hallam arrived. Tomorrow was his final day with the team, and Calladine resolved to try and make these last days as pleasant as possible for the young man. With a smile, he asked Nigel to find any records on the database relating to Kyle and Flora.

"Fancy a pint in the Wheatsheaf tomorrow?" he said to the young DC. "We should do something to mark your last day with us."

"Okay, great idea," Nigel said.

His enthusiasm made Calladine feel guilty. Perhaps all the lad had needed was a friendly face and to feel included. He took his coffee, went back into his office and closed the door. He'd go over the statements in the Flora Appleton case again before he decided on his next move.

They'd taken DNA from everyone involved. So was this the work of a stranger, or someone clever enough never to have crossed their path before? Fat chance they had of getting him if it was. They had nothing but a couple of drops of blood.

"Here you are, sir." Nigel placed a number of printed sheets on Calladine's desk. "Kyle Logan has been brought in four times in total. Each time he got off with warnings. On the third time, uniform rounded up the lot of them — Jack, Dean, Kyle, Flora and Isla Prentice. High as kites, they were. Parents were sent for and once again, they got off with a caution."

Isla Prentice. Calladine suddenly realised that it was quite likely they didn't have her DNA. The boys had had theirs taken that night, when Flora was found, but Isla had gone home by then.

"High as kites, you say? Do we know what they'd taken?"

"Booze and some drug or other. None of them would say what, or where they'd got it from."

"Thanks, Nigel. I think you've hit on something here. I want Isla Prentice and her mother bringing in for a chat. Take a couple of uniforms and go fetch them."

Calladine rang Julian Batho at the Duggan to ask if he could process Isla's DNA quickly, once they had it.

"I'll do what I can," Julian promised. "Roxy has told me about the DNA results with regard to the child's father. And about those items left on the coffee table, I've run the DNA through the database again and there is a match for both Ricky and Sean Hopwood."

That didn't come as any surprise, now that Calladine knew about the relationship. But it did mean they had been in Josie's flat that day. They had never been questioned. At the time, no one had known that they had anything to do with Josie. Too late to speak to Sean now, and it was doubtful Ricky would recall much, if anything.

Isla first, and then Calladine decided he would have to speak to Josie. He couldn't put it off any longer.

* * *

Calladine decided he'd speak to Isla and her mother with Ruth. "We will have to get them to agree to have Isla's DNA taken. You will be helpful on that score. If Isla does have something to hide, she will be reluctant. We have to get her mother on side."

But Joan Prentice wasn't in the best of moods. She was annoyed at being brought to the station. "Everyone on our street will think we're nothing but common criminals! What is so urgent that you couldn't simply come round like before?"

They were in the soft interview room. Calladine asked the uniformed constable to get them some tea. "It's my fault. I do apologise," he began. "But there was an omission made on the night Flora's body was found, and we need to put it right straight away."

Joan Prentice frowned. "What do you mean? What omission? Isla has told you everything she knows."

"Everyone who had anything to do with that car gave a sample of their DNA, but because Isla wasn't there, she was missed out."

"I don't understand. She's done nothing wrong. Why would you want her DNA?"

Ruth smiled at her. "It's purely for elimination purposes, Mrs Prentice. We eliminate any trace of Flora's,

Isla's and the lads' DNA, then what we're left with is possibly that of the killer."

"I see." She looked doubtfully at her daughter. "What does it involve?"

"It's very simple," Ruth assured her. "A mouth swab, that's all."

"And then we're done?"

Calladine leaned towards Isla. "I do have a couple of questions. Not about Flora's murder, but something else. A while ago you were brought here with Kyle and the others. Do you remember, Isla?"

Isla looked away. She didn't look happy with any of this. But he had to ask her about the drugs they'd taken, and where they'd got them from. If her mother hadn't known, then it was hard luck.

But she did. Joan Prentice looked straight at him. "I know what you're referring to. Flora Appleton could be a right little so and so at times. Chasing after the boys, getting my Isla into bother. That stuff they all took was down to her. Flora got it for them."

Calladine looked at Isla, who nodded.

"They were friends, but they had their moments," her mother continued. "I didn't say anything before, Inspector, because the poor girl had been killed. I would have preferred to leave well alone. But if you're going to bring up all that stuff with the drugs, then you need to know."

"Know what, Mrs Prentice?"

"Flora Appleton was a bully. You ask her poor mother. Get her to show you the bruises. Hurt my Isla too, she did, and all over that Hopwood lad, waste of space that he is."

Isla nudged her mother. "It was nothing, Mum."

What did the girl want to hide? Calladine wondered.

"It wasn't nothing. She could have broken your nose," Joan Prentice said indignantly. "Isla came home in a dreadful state, and all because she didn't do what Flora wanted. There was blood all down her clothes. Her nose was so swollen I thought I was going to have to take her to A & E."

"Want to tell us what happened, Isla?" Ruth asked gently.

"Nowt. It were all a mistake. My mum doesn't understand." Isla was uncomfortable, fidgety. She kept nudging her mother. She obviously wasn't happy with this conversation.

The flush that had just come to her cheeks told Calladine just how important this could be.

Joan Prentice brushed her daughter's hand from her arm. "I understand violence well enough, and Flora was one violent girl."

"When did this happen?" asked Calladine.

"Just over a week ago," Joan Prentice said.

"It were longer than that, Mum, more like a month."

The girl's flush deepened. She was lying. Calladine smiled at her. "Okay, thanks for that."

It was enough for now. He needed that DNA test doing. Only then would he be able to voice his suspicions. "Helps to give us a more rounded picture." He nodded at Ruth.

"I'll sort that mouth swab."

* * *

Mother and daughter had left, and Ruth and Calladine were alone. "Fighting, blood, bad feeling between those two girls. You see where this is going, don't you?" said Ruth.

"I'd be the first to agree if it wasn't for one big problem."

He saw Ruth's puzzled look and sighed. "How heavy is Isla Prentice? How strong do you reckon she is?"

"Why does that matter? Two girls fighting, one lands the other a lucky blow. Loses her temper and stabs her."

"Flora was found in the boot of a car. A car parked a good few metres away from where she was killed. How does that happen, given that Isla must be five foot nothing in her stockinged feet, and all of eight stone?"

"She had help!" Ruth's eyes widened.

"Exactly. And that's why those lads were so cagey. One or more of them helped Isla to hide Flora's body."

Ruth looked dubious. "It's a leap, and we have no proof."

"I'm taking that swab to the Duggan myself and then I'll go and see Josie Wilkins. Julian will get Isla's DNA processed quickly. We'll soon know if it's her blood. Then we will challenge the others."

There was a knock on his office door. It was Nigel Hallam.

"Result!" he announced proudly. "The Land Registry have finally come through with something useful. For thirty years prior to the disappearance of Jessica Wilkins, Beardsell Terrace belonged to a Nora Morley."

Calladine shook his head. "I don't know that name."

"I dug a little deeper. Nora Morley was Sean Hopwood's grandmother. Apparently, he lived there with her for most of his childhood."

"Thanks, Nigel. Good work."

"He put her ashes in the house where he'd been safe and happy," Ruth said.

"Looks that way. He took care with how they were stored. Packed silk fabric around the jar, and left a crucifix hanging around it."

"He cared for the little girl."

"He was her father, Ruth. All we have to do now is find out what happened."

Chapter 33

Calladine felt miserable. This wasn't going to be easy. The case had dogged him for years. He needed to put an end to it, but was that likely to happen? Despite knowing about Sean, there were still gaps. Who cremated the child, for example? How was that even done? And how much did the two sisters know?

He had decided to visit Josie alone. He knocked on the door. He could hear a dog barking in one of the neighbouring flats. Kids were back playing along the deck. The place was noisy, dirty. Calladine shuddered. Tracy should have got them out of here years ago.

"What now?" Josie said.

Same old Josie. Tracksuit bottoms, an old T-shirt and battered trainers. Her hair looked as if it hadn't been washed in days and hung in a limp mass around her pale face.

"Can I come in?" he said.

Wordlessly, she moved aside.

The place was much the same as always. There was a pile of dirty pots festering in the kitchen sink and a load of dirty washing by the machine. Calladine decided to refuse tea if she offered. He didn't even want to sit down, but this might take a while.

"Have you found out what happened to my Jess?" Josie asked in a small voice.

"No, not all of it."

What to say now? How did he tell this damaged woman that her child had been shot through the head and her body burned? He would start with something less controversial, and lead up to the awful bit gradually.

"You knew Sean Hopwood years ago, before he became a moneylender."

Josie stood and stared at him, her arms folded around her thin frame. Eventually she said, "So what? He used to be okay before he had money and that big house."

"Sean was killed, Josie, you know that. We did tests, and we now know that he was Jessica's father."

The expression on Josie's face didn't change. She started to pace the room. The only sound was her loose-fitting slippers scuffing against the carpet. "What difference does it make who Jess's father was?"

"You never said anything back then. Why keep it a secret?"

"Tracy said I had to."

"Did she say why?"

"Tracy always knows what's best."

"Do you remember that afternoon, Josie?" Her face pulled into a frown. "Was Jessica in that pushchair when you went to the park?"

The question hung in the air and reverberated around Calladine's head. It was the big one. Josie was weeping now, clutching a towel and holding it to her face.

"I don't know. I didn't even look. I was off my face on smack. But I do know something weird happened," she said.

Calladine could see that she was trying to remember. Trying to dredge the hidden memories up from some safe, forgotten place in her head.

"It was something bad, but Tracy would never tell me."

"But you went to the park. You sat on a bench. People saw you."

"I don't remember any of it." She turned to face him. "Despite what I might have said at the time, I never did."

* * *

Calladine stayed with Josie until a family liaison officer arrived to sit with her. She was in no state to be left alone. From what Josie had told him, her sister Tracy was the one he needed to talk to. But it was late in the afternoon. He rang social services, but she'd left for the day, and they refused to give out her mobile number.

Calladine wanted to tackle Tracy and get to the truth, but he still had the Isla Prentice statement to figure out. If she had killed Flora, then someone must have helped her to move and hide the body. What was the betting that person was Kyle Logan? Hence the urgency to torch the car.

Calladine asked uniform to find Tracy and bring her down to the station. Over the top? He didn't think so. For years she'd been withholding vital information about the death of an infant.

"We need to speak to Kyle Logan again," he told the team. He looked at Nigel. "Take a uniform and go and fetch him. "I think Isla killed Flora. The DNA from those drops of blood will confirm it, but in the meantime we need to find out who helped her."

"And you think that was Kyle?" asked Ruth.

"Yes, and possibly someone else."

"Ricky?"

"I'm not sure about Ricky Hopwood. He comes across as straight enough, but there is something he's keeping back."

"How did you get on with Josie?"

"She knows nothing that will help. Tracy is the one we need to speak to now. I'm having her brought in."

"Frank Chadwick is in a bad way. He's been readmitted to hospital. The paramedics who took him in think he's had a heart attack. Poor man. He's really been through the mill."

Calladine looked at her. "He took a knife and killed Sean Hopwood."

"Extreme provocation, I would say. Look what Hopwood did to Annie." She returned his gaze.

"Tracy Wilkins is downstairs, guv," Joyce called out.

"I'll go and speak to her."

* * *

Calladine wasn't looking forward to this. Tracy was very different from her sister, tough and intelligent. She wouldn't give anything away unless she absolutely had to.

"Why am I here?"

She was staring at him, her expression a mixture of mistrust and something else. It wasn't fear, more like wariness. Tracy would be wondering what he might have found out.

Calladine sat down facing her. "The day Jessica disappeared. I know she was never at the park, so where was she?"

"You're deluded! Of course she was. Josie took her for a walk."

"Josie was drugged up to the eyeballs. She never even looked in that pushchair." Calladine looked straight into her eyes. "Jessica was shot through the head. Shot, Tracy!"

"How can you know that?"

The caution had evaporated. There was very real fear in her voice now.

"Are you saying that wasn't what happened?"

Tracy Wilkins closed her eyes and shook her head. "It was an accident, a fluke," she whispered.

"Who did the gun belong to?"

"Sean Hopwood."

"We also know that Sean was Jessica's father. Another little titbit you kept from us back then."

"Josie didn't want anyone to know. Sean was just starting up in the moneylending business and she was well aware of how he operated."

"Who killed Jessica?"

Tracy sighed heavily and leaned back in the chair. "Ricky did."

Calladine was staggered. At first he wasn't sure he'd heard her right. "Ricky was only a child himself."

"Jess was just a couple of months off being two and Ricky was almost four. We were in Josie's flat. Ricky and Jess were playing hide and seek. Sean had left some stuff of his in a cupboard, and had told Josie not to go near it. But Ricky crawled inside to hide, and he found the gun." She paused. Calladine could see the tears welling in her eyes. "I had my hands full with Josie. She'd taken something, and she'd been drinking. I was trying to bring her round. Next thing, I heard the shot."

At this, Tracy broke down completely. The stress of having to keep this secret for so many years had finally overtaken her.

"Sorry," she said finally, dabbing her eyes. "I found little Jess on the bedroom floor, covered in blood. Ricky still had the gun in his hand. He was waving it about, playing some cowboy game or other. He was a kid. He didn't know what he'd done." She looked at Calladine. "I don't think he knows to this day!"

"Then what happened?"

"Josie didn't even wake up. I wrapped Jess in a blanket and hid her. When Sean came back he was completely devastated. He laid into Josie, but she was oblivious. I had to stop him from beating Ricky black and blue. He was a child, he'd no idea what had happened. After a lot of shouting, he decided to take Jess away. I never did know what he did with her, and I never asked."

"He burned her," said Calladine. "Put her ashes in an expensive jar and sealed it up behind his granny's fireplace in a house on Beardsell Terrace."

Tracy nodded. "He was brought up there. It's where he was happiest. He had crap parents. If his granny hadn't died when he was in his teens, if she'd been around to guide him, I'm sure Sean would have been a different man."

"How come Josie never knew any of this?"

"She finally woke up sometime in the mid-afternoon. The pushchair was in the hall all ready. It was a hot day, the hood was up and I'd fixed the sun shade on earlier. Josie must have presumed Jess was in there asleep. She took it and went off out without saying a word." Tracy stopped talking for a moment. "Next thing I knew, they were saying Jess had been stolen from her pushchair in the park. The rest, you know."

"You've kept this to yourself all these years?"

"Yes, I have. I had to protect Josie, and Ricky too initially. I never gave a toss about Sean. It was his gun. He hid it in Josie's cupboard, stupid bastard. He knew there were kids around. I could never see what good telling the truth would do."

Chapter 34

Saturday

"So now we know." Ruth set down Tracy Wilkins's statement on Calladine's desk. "What are you going to charge her with?"

"That's up to the CPS. I wouldn't know where to start." Calladine felt weary. He'd been unable to sleep the previous night. The Jessica Wilkins case had finally been solved, but it still bothered him. He'd imagined that once he knew what really happened to that little girl, he'd feel a weight lift. But all he could think was that but for Sean Hopwood, it never would have happened.

"How did Hopwood burn her body?" Ruth asked. "I know it's gruesome, but isn't it a difficult thing to do?"

"The body was small, the bones still forming. I imagine if you had a fire that burned hot enough and for long enough, it would be possible. That huge house the Hopwoods live in is Victorian. At one time there will have been an industrial-sized boiler in the cellar. I'd ask Julian about it. I'm sure he'll be only too pleased to explain." Calladine had had enough. They had crossed off the Sean

Hopwood killing, and the disappearance of Jessica Wilkins was sorted. All he wanted now was to find Flora Appleton's killer, and then they could call it a day.

"Are you going to tell Josie?"

"No. Tracy is. I'll go and see her next week. Let the truth settle first. She won't be happy, and this is bound to cause a rift between the two sisters."

Rocco popped his head around Calladine's office door. "Kyle Logan is in the interview room."

"Want to join me?" Calladine asked Ruth.

"You think he helped Isla to hide Flora's body?"

"Yes, I do."

"Why would he, Tom, if he didn't have anything to do with killing her? It's just stupid."

Calladine shrugged. "Let's see what he has to say first."

* * *

Kyle Logan was as stroppy as ever. He slapped the flat of his hands on the table. "What am I doing here — again! I've done nowt. Go and pick on some other bugger."

Calladine ignored his angry words. He sat down, facing Kyle. "Tell me about the night Flora was killed."

"It wasn't me. I wasn't there. Jesus! What does it take to make you see?"

Calladine smiled. "I don't think it was you that killed Flora, Kyle, so relax. But I do think you were there."

"How d'you reckon that?"

"Because someone had to help the killer stuff Flora's body in the boot of Marshal's car, that's why."

The lad looked puzzled. His eyes moved from Calladine to Ruth and then back to Calladine. "Clever bugger, aren't you, copper?"

"Come on then, Kyle. Tell us what happened," Ruth said.

"No! I want a solicitor. I don't have to talk to you. I know my rights."

This was getting them nowhere. "Okay, Kyle, we'll get someone for you."

Ruth and Calladine left him tapping his foot impatiently.

"What makes you so sure it was him?" Ruth asked.

"He wanted to torch the car."

She looked at him. "And that's it?"

"He was working only a few metres away that night."

Nigel looked up when they entered the incident room. "Guv, Professor Batho says will you ring him."

It was Saturday. Nigel's last day.

"I'll ring him in my office."

Julian had processed the DNA sample from Isla. As Calladine had suspected, he confirmed that the blood found at the scene belonged to her. It was looking as if they finally had their killer.

Calladine went out and called to Rocco. "The unknown blood at the scene was Isla's. Bring her in."

Ruth looked at him. "Her mother won't be pleased. She'll have to come too. Isla is only sixteen."

"And she can have a solicitor, anything it takes. But she did it, Ruth, and she must be charged!"

* * *

Joan Prentice glared at him. "I hope you've got your facts right, Inspector. Dragging my Isla in here at the weekend! You've got some nerve."

Calladine ignored this remark and turned to the girl. "Isla, can you tell me what your blood is doing at the scene of Flora's murder?"

The duty solicitor cleared his throat, leaned towards Isla and whispered something in her ear.

Isla stuck her nose in the air. "No comment!"

Calladine gave her an encouraging smile. "It will go better for you if you speak to me, Isla. We have evidence that places you at the scene. We know you had help to hide the body too. That person will tell us the truth."

That shook her. She looked at her mother.

"Mum . . . ? What do I say now?"

Joan Prentice looked from Calladine to the solicitor. "Is this evidence good enough to stand up in court? Or is this some trick to get a confession out of my daughter?"

"We have solid forensic evidence, Mrs Prentice. Whatever Isla might say to the contrary, she was there."

Joan Prentice sat back in her seat. "In that case, speak to them, Isla. Tell them what happened."

Isla shook her head. "They'll lock me up!" she cried.

"But they know. They have evidence. It will go better for you if you help them. Please, Isla, tell them the truth."

Isla spoke angrily, her eyes on the floor. "I hated Flora. She had everything. She had her freedom, money, but most of all she had Ricky. It wasn't fair. She was a bitch to him."

So this was all down to jealousy, Calladine realised. "What happened, Isla?"

"I saw them together that night. Flora had made Ricky get her drugs. His brother knew people to go to, and Ricky found out their contact details. Sean never gave Ricky much money, he was always broke. Flora said that if he could get something to sell, she'd help him. She said they could make a lot of money."

"Is that why they met?"

"I think so. But Flora wouldn't give Ricky the money. She took the drugs and told him to get lost. He was upset. She felt nothing for him, and I couldn't stand that. She had it all, it wasn't fair. I'd wanted Ricky for ages. I saw red. I didn't see why Flora should get away with it. I chased after her. I was going to take the money off her, give it to Ricky, but we ended up fighting."

Ruth said, "You had a knife with you. Did you intend to hurt someone?"

"I always took a knife when I went out at night."

Isla's mother tutted.

Isla turned to her mother. "It's not safe. I keep one of the steak knives in my pocket."

"What did you do with the knife?" Calladine asked.

"It's at home. I didn't know what to do with it. I'm going on holiday to Scotland in a couple of weeks with school. I thought I might drop it in a loch or something. Make sure it's never found."

"So where is it now?"

"It's in a plastic bag under my bed."

Calladine nodded at the uniformed officer stood by the door. "Tell DC Rockliffe to retrieve it, and get it to the Duggan," he ordered. The knife would prove forensically what Isla was telling them.

"This fight you had, did Flora hurt you?"

"She bust my nose."

That was where the blood had come from.

"Did you send that text to Flora's mum?"

She nodded. "I didn't want people looking for her. I knew Dolly wouldn't question it. Flora'd told her she wanted to go to that festival."

"Do you still have Flora's mobile?"

"Yes, that's at home with the knife."

"Who helped you hide the body, Isla?"

"Kyle. He was having a fag outside. He heard the noise. When he saw what had happened, he carried Flora across and put her in the boot of that car."

"That's why you were scared the night the lads wanted to take the car, why you left. You knew what was inside. What about Ricky? Was he party to any of this?"

She shook her head. "He also thought Flora had gone off to the festival." Tears were rolling down her cheeks. "After Flora left him, Kyle took him into the pub and got him a drink."

"So why did Kyle help you?"

"He made me give him money. He said he'd get rid of the body and say nothing if I paid him. I've been paying him off ever since. That night we found Flora, he was angry. He wanted the lads to do one and leave it. I knew why. That was the night he was going to take the car up on the moors and set it alight."

Chapter 35

DCI Rhona Birch strode into the incident room. "You've cleared the decks! Jolly good, Calladine. What are we doing about Hallam?"

"Drink in the Wheatsheaf in about ten minutes. The others have already gone across."

"The girl confessed and you got your evidence, well done."

Praise indeed, Calladine managed a smile in return.

"I'll see you over there then."

Calladine shuddered. That was all he needed. He was knackered, and entertaining Rhona Birch didn't feature in his to-do list.

Ruth came in and stood beside him. "Rocco has asked Alice to join us. You okay with that?"

"It's fine by me. She'll be part of the team come Monday."

"What about Julian? Is he coming?"

"Rocco asked him and Roxy, why?"

"Thought I'd ask Julian about the fire thing. How long, and what you'd need to burn a body, albeit a small one."

"Ghoulish thinking, Bayliss, not like you at all!"

"Just curious." Ruth handed him a card. "Sign this. We've got him a bottle of scotch too."

Calladine began cleaning up the board. "It's been a tough few days. All I want now is a quiet weekend."

Ruth smiled. "It's half over, already."

"What are you doing?"

"I'm off on Monday, so tomorrow me and Jake are going to look at that school in Dorset."

Calladine's heart sank. "Thought you were dead set against the move?"

"I am, but there's no harm in looking."

Calladine tossed the paperwork he'd been shuffling onto the nearest desk. "I need a drink. This place is going to pot."

"Calm down. It's just a visit. No one is going anywhere permanently."

Now Calladine felt guilty. He was doing his spoilt kid bit again. But then again, Ruth might like the place. What then? Jake was a very important part of her life. He would try very hard to persuade her.

"It's about tactics," she told him. "Once I see the place I'll know what I'm up against. Don't worry, I'm not going to be impressed by fancy buildings and lovely countryside, we've got all that round here. I'm showing willing, that's all."

They set off down the stairs. "I've told you, leave and I'll retire."

Ruth grinned. "What you need is a new woman in your life."

"Funny you should say that. Don't think I've mentioned it, but I've got a new neighbour. Layla, she's called. Nice too. Last night she brought round a homemade cottage pie. We shared that and a bottle of red. She doesn't start her new job until next week. My usual dog minder is away, so I gave her a key and she's been walking Sam for me too."

Ruth nudged him. "You're a dark horse, Calladine. You never said a word."

He winked at her. "Don't tell you everything."

"So you're well over Shez now? Didn't last, did it? Mind you, she was far too flash for you, all high heels, designer clothes and red lippy. What do you think? Is this new one a keeper?"

"How am I supposed to know that? I hardly know the woman!"

"She's cooking your tea, got a key to your house and walking your dog. There must be something."

"You know what it's like. Women come and go."

"They certainly do where you're concerned, Tom. Do you never fancy settling down? Meeting someone and trying hard to make it for keeps?"

"God no, where's the fun in that," he nudged her.

"So when do we get to meet her?"

"Thought I might bring her round to yours one night next week. You could do your spag bol, and I'll try to make Jake see the error of his ways."

"Sounds like a plan. Wednesday suit you?"

THE END

Thank you for reading this book. If you enjoyed it please leave feedback on Amazon, and if there is anything we missed or you have a question about then please get in touch. The author and publishing team appreciate your feedback and time reading this book.

Our email is office@joffebooks.com

www.joffebooks.com

ALSO BY HELEN H. DURRANT

CALLADINE & BAYLISS MYSTERIES
DEAD WRONG
DEAD SILENT
DEAD LIST
DEAD LOST
DEAD & BURIED
DEAD NASTY
DEAD JEALOUS

DI GRECO
DARK MURDER
DARK HOUSES
DARK TRADE

24490241R00134

Printed in Great Britain
by Amazon